Who Owns Tomorrow?

By

Larry Morris

This work is dedicated to my wife, Michelle, for her continued love and support. She continues to be my first stop for story content and my best critic.

Special dedication to Wayne Skaggs. This, my first work since his passing, was born on his deck in many conversations on the nature of time. I regret that he isn't around to see it in print.

Many thanks to Judy, Allan, Cathy, Carl, Dawn, Michelle, Leo and Sharon for their reviewing efforts.

Special thanks to Leo for the title. It wouldn't have been the same book without it.

Who Owns Tomorrow?

Chapter 1
Event minus 24 hours
Residence of Colonel Karen Stiles

Karen sat at the kitchen table with her morning coffee, looking out the window past the deck, relishing the new snow. It was still pretty early, at least for everyone else, and the sun was not yet fully up. Shadows were just starting to creep from the trees, and the new-fallen snow was beginning to glisten. This was her favorite time of the day, before anyone else moved and spoiled the scene. She could sit here for hours this time of year and just watch the snow and the small animals that would scurry around the neighborhood.

This ritual was the only thing that made it bearable when Brian was gone on a long deployment. When his submarine deployed it was usually for a three month trip, and she never knew where he was or if he would be back on time. Or even be back at all. Communications to and from the nuclear sub fleet was strictly monitored and family conversations during deployment were frowned upon.

A cottontail had found the hole in the back fence and hopped across the backyard. When it was even with the deck and the window Karen looked out of, it stopped and sat up and looked right at her. White on white. This was an everyday occurrence in the winters where she had grown up in northern Indiana, close to the Michigan border, but not as often here just outside the nation's capital. She took advantage of these moments whenever they happened.

The cottontail hopped off, back through the hole in the fence, and Karen continued to sit and watch.

But, as always, eventually, she had to get to work. There were things going on she was responsible for, and as much as she liked how it was right here, she knew she couldn't stay.

She sipped her coffee and watched the wind swirl the powdery snow when she had the overwhelming feeling that this was somehow vaguely familiar. Not familiar as in she did this all the time, but familiar as in she had done exactly this before.

That was when she first heard the noise. It didn't sound like anything in particular at first, just a noise. But the more she strained to listen, the more it actually sounded like someone softly calling her name.

She stood up and held her breath and cocked her head in the direction of the sound. She tried to concentrate to make sure what she thought she was hearing was real.

"Karen," the voice said. "Karen, can you hear me?" It was a woman's voice, and it sounded like it was coming from behind her.

She grabbed the table with her left hand and sat her coffee down hard enough to spill some on the table. She spun around to look behind her.

Who Owns Tomorrow?

"Is someone there?" she asked out loud, her eyes darting around the kitchen. There was no one else there. Just her and Sebastian.

She slowly moved toward the short hallway between the kitchen and the front foyer. Sebastian watched her from the safety of his bed in the corner of the kitchen. He yawned and stretched. He got up and turned around a couple of times in true cat fashion before he finally sat on his haunches and continued to watch her. He had been asleep and had not heard the voice the first time, so he was curious about what she was doing.

Karen got to the hallway and snapped on the light. It was empty. She touched a small picture frame on its lower left corner and it tilted down to reveal a concealed compartment. She reached in and pulled out the Sig P229 with her right hand. Not many things would stay standing after a couple of rounds from her trusted .40 caliber.

She pushed open the door to the small powder room on her right. It was empty.

"What's going on here, Bastian?" she asked. She looked over her shoulder at the cat and he tilted his head to one side. "You're supposed to tell me when something out of the ordinary is happening. I think you slept too long this morning."

Then she heard the voice again. This time it was clearer, and it was obvious it was coming from the foyer.

"Karen, please, can you hear me?"

Sebastian heard it this time and sat up a little straighter. He looked at Karen, trying to take his cue from his mistress. Not much flustered the big tom, but this was a voice where there shouldn't be one. He was familiar enough with his owner's routine to know she was supposed to be alone at this time of the morning when Brian was gone.

Karen reached her free hand around the wall into the foyer and flipped the light switch while she was still standing in the little hallway. She pulled back the hammer on the Sig and peeked quickly around the corner. Light flooded the small foyer, split into a rainbow by the cut glass of the front door. She surveyed the small space from the hallway, taking her time now. There was no one there. Just a hat rack, the front door and an old antique sideboard with a large, beveled-glass mirror. She could see the alarm-monitoring unit on the wall by the front door, and it was still armed. Just the way she had left it last night before she went to bed. No one else was in the house.

She walked over to the sideboard and looked in the mirror. Sebastian startled her as he rubbed up against her leg and she almost fell backwards.

"Damn it, Bastian," she said. "Let me know when you're about to scare the shit out of me." She bent down to pet the cat, and the voice came again.

"Karen ...," was all the voice said.

Who Owns Tomorrow?

When Karen stood back up and looked at the mirror in the sideboard, she thought she saw something besides her own reflection. She thought she saw another *her* looking back. It was fuzzy and wavy like something you would see through a heat wave, but it sure looked like her. Of course, that was crazy. It must have just been her imagination.

She backed up to the doorway into the hallway and grabbed the door frame to keep from falling. Her head was swimming, and for a minute she was sure she was about to faint. But she held on. She didn't know what this was, but it scared the daylights out of her.

She collected herself and stepped back into the foyer in front of the sideboard. The image and the voice had faded, and just the mirror remained. She stood there for a full 10 minutes watching. Waiting for something else to happen. Nothing did.

She decocked the Sig and put it back in its holder inside the picture frame and closed the frame.

She shook her head and retrieved her coffee from the kitchen table and wiped up the spill with a couple of paper towels. She stood at the kitchen table sipping coffee and thinking about what had just happened. She really had no choice. She pulled her phone from her pocket and sent a 911 text to a local number and looked at her watch. She figured she had about 15 minutes before they showed up, so she turned off the alarm, and headed upstairs for a quick shower. Her front door had a

[8]

keypad lock instead of a key lock and the folks who were going to respond to her 911 request had the code to get into the house. On the way, she stopped at the wet bar on the second floor for a scotch. It may have been early, but coffee by itself just wasn't going to cut it today.

Not knowing what else to do at the moment, Sebastian followed her upstairs, talking all the way.

She paused at the bedroom door and took a long pull from the scotch. Something about the encounter this morning was nagging at her. Not just how strange it was; there was, of course, that. But there was something else. If she held her head just right and closed her eyes, she could remember … something. Again, the feeling that this was all so familiar. But then it was all gone, just a fleeting memory fragment. She finished the scotch in one swallow and headed into the bedroom for a shower.

Who Owns Tomorrow?

Karen worked for DARPA (The Defense Advanced Research Projects Agency) in Arlington and commuted every day from a little community called West Falls Church. The entire neighborhood was mostly DARPA. She had been with them for over 10 years and had led several projects, all related to high-energy particle physics. They had recruited her right out of college and she'd been there ever since. She was in charge of the STO (Strategic Technology Office), the youngest person ever to head the department. The current project she was working on was a high-energy shield to protect personnel, groups of vehicles, or buildings. They were about a day away from the first major test, so everyone was on pins and needles. This was a very highly visible project. That's what they said when you really couldn't afford to screw it up.

Even though most of the people in her department were military, no one stood on ceremony at the facilities. In fact, they preferred not to stand out as a military installation, but would rather blend into the Arlington countryside along with all the other high-tech firms. She was a full colonel and was up for her first star this year, but she was tired. Not so much of the military, but more of the job she did. It was dangerous, and she fully expected on most days not to even make it home. All it took was one little mistake and there would be hell to pay. For more than just her. For most of the world.

Most of the time, she thought of herself as still young. She had thought a couple of times that perhaps the fates were trying to tell her something, she was 40 this year and it was 2040. Just a coincidence? Perhaps, but this morning, more than ever, she thought it might be time to retire.

Who Owns Tomorrow?

She showered and put on comfortable civilian clothes. She was on her way down the stairs when the emergency response team came through the front door.

"Colonel Stiles, I'm Sgt. Adrian Doyle, the Emergency Responder on duty," the clean-cut Army master sergeant said as he walked up to Karen. He was flanked by four lower-ranking technicians, two on either side. "What's the problem?"

Karen looked out the front door. There was a Humvee in the driveway with two armed guards standing beside it.

"It happened this morning while I was having my morning coffee," Karen said. "I was in the kitchen when I heard, …" she paused, "the disturbance."

"Where was it coming from?" the sergeant asked.

"From here, in the foyer. Let's look at the security footage of the incident. It started about 20 minutes before I called."

She headed to a small room just off the kitchen, past Sebastian's bed. Sgt. Doyle and the team followed. Karen unlocked the room, and they all went in. It looked to be perhaps 12 by 12 and was originally intended to be an office. There were four large, flat screens on a small desk flanked by two racks of servers.

"There are the standard cameras and microphones in every room," Karen said. "You can't see them but everything that happens in the house is recorded."

"Where did you say the disturbance was?" Sgt. Doyle asked. He sat down at the center screen, signed into the system and brought up all the camera feeds.

"The foyer," Karen said and pointed to the right camera feed. "It was the mirror on the sideboard."

Sebastian had come downstairs while they were going through video files and sat in the doorway behind them.

"Mauw," he said.

Karen jumped. "Jesus, Sebastian. Will you stop sneaking up on me?"

The big tom looked up at her and purred, happy just to hear her voice.

"Here it is," Sgt. Doyle said. He had positioned the two videos, the one from the foyer and the one from the kitchen, to the proper time and paused them. Karen leaned in over his shoulder to watch the feeds. This would be new information for her as well. She hadn't seen any of this footage so far. The four aides leaned in as well to watch as he started both videos at the same time.

"Karen," the voice said. *"Karen, can you hear me?"* It was the first voice she heard while she was still in the kitchen. It came from the mirror on the sideboard. Adrian stopped both feeds and backed up the foyer feed.

Who Owns Tomorrow?

Before he started it again, he zoomed the playback in as far as it would go. They were centered on the mirror, almost full screen.

"Karen," the voice said. *"Karen, can you hear me?"* Karen took a step back with her hand over her mouth.

"Jesus," she whispered through her hand. "That's me." They were looking at Karen on the security screen, no question about it. She was in civilian clothes and sat behind a large table. Sgt. Doyle looked up at her and then back at the screen. She had a different hair style and seemed a little older, maybe a little more tired and haggard, but it was her. Her clothes were dirty and torn in a couple of places, but the Karen in the video was clearly wearing the same outfit she currently had on.

Around her was a disaster. Neither of them recognized the surroundings. It didn't look like DARPA headquarters as far as they could tell, but wherever it was, it was pretty much destroyed. Rubble, broken glass, small fires and smoke everywhere. There were people standing behind her but it was difficult to tell who they were. It seemed like all the available light was focused on her.

"This isn't possible," Karen said. "I don't see how this makes any sense at all." She was still standing a few paces back from the desk, shaking her head back and forth. Sebastian made a small noise by her feet and she picked him up and held him close to her.

[14]

Sgt. Doyle stopped both playback feeds. "Well, it isn't my job to make sense out of it, that's a bit over my pay grade. I'm here to verify that we do have an issue, set up more sophisticated recording equipment if needed and notify headquarters if I think it's warranted. Trust me. I think it's warranted."

He keyed the mic at his shoulder, "Trey, get the cameras and servers in here." Then he pulled a cell phone out of his pocket, dialed a number and said, "This is Sgt. Adrian Doyle, ER 80742761. Who's on for level-2 support this morning?" He listened for a few seconds then said, "Okay, have Dr. Sheffield and his team report to me at my position as soon as possible. I'm declaring a level-2 event." He hung up.

"Dr. Sheffield?" Karen asked. "I know him, he's a senior physicist on the overall support team. I thought he just consulted."

"He does," Sgt. Doyle said. "But his real responsibility is to provide support when a level-2 event is declared. We have four teams that provide this support, and he and his team are still on from last night."

"Exactly what is level-2 support?" Karen asked as the two guards that were outside showed up in the little office with armloads of equipment. They went back outside after dropping off the equipment.

"Let's get out of their way," Sgt. Doyle said as he guided her out of the small room and back into the kitchen. Karen put Sebastian in his bed and made another pot of coffee. "Level-2 is called at the discretion of the on-site Emergency Responder. It's usually called when the ER sees or hears something he can't explain or resolve on his own."

"How often is a level-2 called?"

"Well, I've been doing this job at the STO for over five years, and this is the first time I've called one."

The techs were moving from room to room setting up new high-definition cameras and adding new servers, so Sgt. Doyle and Karen sat down at the kitchen table and had a cup of coffee.

"It will take a good 30 minutes for the level-2 team to get here, and then it's pretty much a waiting game. From what we understand, they want whatever event we're dealing with to repeat itself so they can do on-site analysis."

"So we really have no frame of reference with which to compare this event, do we?" Karen asked.

"Not from me or my team," Sgt. Doyle said. "Dr. Sheffield may have more input. My sense is that he's been at this a long time."

The techs reported in that they had finished all the upgrades.

"Excuse me," Sgt. Doyle said. He got up and left to check out the install.

Karen was an accomplished physicist herself and knew that with the right amount of power and an unlimited budget for equipment and research, almost anything was possible. *Almost* being the operative word. But she had no idea what this event could represent. It didn't make any sense to her at all. Seeing herself in that mirror frightened her like never before. It was her, but then again, not really. The *her* in the mirror looked like she had lived through hell. As far as she could tell, physics had nothing to do with this. It seemed like a bad nightmare to her.

Sgt. Doyle came back into the kitchen with Dr. Sheffield and they both sat down at the table. Sgt. Doyle did the introductions.

"Karen," Dr. Sheffield said, "has anything like this ever happened to you before? Either here at home, at DARPA or anywhere else?"

"No, this is a first for me. I'm still not sure what's going on."

"What is your team working on at the office?" He already knew this, but wanted to hear it from her.

Karen looked at Sgt. Doyle and the support team and then back at Dr. Sheffield.

"Guys, give us the room for a few minutes here, will you?" Dr. Sheffield asked the rest of the support team.

As soon as they cleared out, Karen said "Sorry, it's habit. You can't be too careful."

"I understand, it is the correct protocol."

"We're working on a high-energy shield for personnel and small equipment, vehicles and the like, even up to small buildings. Project Achilles. We can't make it any bigger right now, maybe for planes or ships, due to power consumption issues. Bigger means more power, more power means it's not portable anymore and the costs get prohibitive."

"So, you've run tests already?"

"No, everything so far has been all math and simulations. We're scheduled to run our first test tomorrow, just under 24 hours from now."

"Small test or full power?"

"It's scheduled to be a full-power test run, why?"

"I don't know yet, I'm just collecting data. Sometimes you don't know you need something until you need it. Most of the time, I just collect data."

"Has this ever happened before?" Karen asked.

"Let's wait until we get a little more data before we start talking about what this is or whether it's ever happened before. Sometimes, these things turn out to be not much of anything."

"Then you haven't seen the security tapes yet, have you?"

"No, I haven't," Dr. Sheffield said. "That was my next stop." He stood up and called Sgt. Doyle back in. "Let's see what you've got on the recordings."

They went into the little office and were there no more than five minutes. Dr. Sheffield looked a little disturbed when they came out. He sat back down with Karen at the kitchen table.

"I've never seen anything like this before," he said. "I have no idea what it is."

"Do you think it's related to what we're doing at the office?" Karen asked.

"The only clue we have so far is that it is you in the mirror. Beyond that, until we get more information, I can't speculate."

"Karen?" the voice asked again. "Karen, are you there?"

Everybody stood up. Sebastian raised his head up off his paws and looked at Karen.

The voice was back and sounded stronger this time. Now they were sure; it even sounded like Karen.

"Okay, let's move quietly but quickly to the foyer," Dr. Sheffield said. "Sgt. Doyle, post guards at both the front and back door, until I tell you to relieve them."

Sgt. Doyle moved quickly to post guards while Karen and Dr. Sheffield went into the foyer. There were a few chairs already set up directly in front of the sideboard, at mirror height. There were a few other people Karen didn't recognize already seated with pen and paper. She and Dr. Sheffield sat down in the two vacant seats in the front and Dr. Sheffield started a separate, high-speed recorder that was standing by on a tripod.

The *Karen* in the mirror was back. Looking just as disheveled as before, perhaps a little more so. If that was possible. She didn't seem to be looking into a camera, but she did somehow seem to actually be staring at them in the foyer. Karen and Dr. Sheffield couldn't figure out what she was doing; it appeared she was just staring at them.

It became obvious she couldn't see or hear them as nothing they did made her react. She was just staring ahead, perhaps looking at something out of their field of view. Something, or someone, was at about the same distance from her as the people in the foyer were from the mirror. Occasionally, she would turn to one side or the other and look at something else, almost like someone else was in the room talking to her. She would listen intently, then nod and turn back to look toward the people in the foyer.

Then she spoke again.

"Karen," she said.

"Colonel Karen Stiles," she said.

"We can't see or hear you, but you should be able to see and hear us. My tech people tell me we are in the correct space and time. Please listen carefully. What I'm about to tell you could very well save the world. If you're not already doing so, please record everything. We don't have much time, and I will not be repeating any of this message. We only have enough power for a few minutes of this transmission. If we get cut off, there may be other messages, but I can't guarantee it."

Chapter 2
Event minus 22 hours
U.S.S. *Tennessee*

Captain Brian Stiles sat in his quarters and updated the ship's log. He was the captain of the U.S.S. *Tennessee*, one of the nuclear ballistic submarines, or boomers, that roamed the Atlantic for the U.S. as part of its nuclear deterrent force. The Ridge Runner, as she was known by the crew, usually carried 16 of the new Trident III D-7 class nuclear-tipped missiles, each with a range of 5,000 nautical miles and a payload of 12 independently targeted warheads, each roughly twenty times the destructive power of the warhead dropped on Hiroshima. All together, it carried a little over 57 megatons of destructive fury, normally. There were at least a dozen of these subs out at all times, and perhaps only a handful of people knew where some of them were. No one ever knew where all of them were at any given moment. That was one of the points of the ballistic sub program.

For the next few days they were on a special deployment to test a new missile propellant, so four of the tubes were holding duds. No payload. The job was to hug the east coast of the U.S. and launch when they got well south of D.C. The missiles were to reach maximum altitude and then target the middle of the Atlantic. No harm, no foul, no explosion.

Even with duds, this process was by no means easy or simple. This was also to be a full test of the procedures for releasing nuclear weapons as well as testing the new propellant. That meant, among other things, that no one on board the ship had the combination to the safe that held the nuclear trigger. That would come with the EAM, Emergency Action Message, that directed the release of the weapons. Without that authorization, and the combination to the safe, there was no way the missiles would, or could, be fired. At least that was the theory.

There were a couple of other surprises the sub was going to test while it was out if it had the opportunity. They were some additional toys that might give them an edge in a real battle. Some of them the crew knew about, some only a handful knew.

If they ever got into a shooting war, the ballistic missiles had to be fired one at a time. The ship couldn't stand the stress of more than that. The crew had all often talked about how many missiles they thought they could get up before being hit themselves. Every nation had the capability to not only determine a nuclear weapon had been launched, but to pinpoint where it came from and fire their own counter-strike weapon within a matter of minutes, if not seconds.

Brian was in the pool for three missiles. Several of the other officers were in for one or two, but no one was in for more than four.

If they had the opportunity to do so, they would dive and maneuver away from the launch position to surface somewhere else and launch again. But that usually took too much time when time was something they didn't have.

Brian hated these test runs, even though he knew they had to be done from time to time. It was just his turn in the bucket. At least this might be a quicker deployment and he could get back to Karen sooner. She was getting tired of what she did and had been talking lately about packing it in and either retiring outright or moving to the civilian sector. She said what they were doing was getting way too dangerous, and she worried about it a lot. She usually never talked much about exactly what it was they were involved in, only once that he could remember.

The radio brought Brian out of his thoughts.

"Captain, Conn."

Brian picked up the mic on the wall by the door to his quarters.

"Conn, Stiles," he replied. "What's up?"

"Sir, can you report to missile silo 16?" the voice asked. "The weapons officer has found a problem."

Brian thought for a moment. *What would the weapons officer be doing at one of the missile silos?* The sub's weapons officer was Lt. Haskins. He had been under Stiles command for over five years and was the best weapons guy Brian had ever met. But everything he did was usually from his main station next to the weapons bays or in the control room. He usually never had to actually touch a missile silo.

"Conn, Stiles, will do," Brian replied. "Have COB meet me there."

COB, or Chief of the Boat, in this case was Master Chief Petty Officer Ryan, a 25-year veteran of the Navy, and he had been on Ballistic submarines for the past seven years. Brian closed his log book and left his quarters. It would take a good five minutes to get to Ballistic Row where the missile silos were.

The last time Brian and Karen had the opportunity to have some extended time alone was four years ago when they both had several days off at the same time. It was only the second time it had happened since they had been married, and the only time Karen had opened up about work.

She talked a little about what they were doing at DARPA that she was involved in. That was four years ago, so it had to be further along by now.

She called it a high-energy shield project. Project Achilles, if he remembered correctly. The idea was to apply massive amounts of power, from where he had no clue, to a new top-secret resonator that would vibrate the atoms of the air around whatever it was you wanted to protect. When they vibrated at a certain frequency, almost everything bounced off of them. Really, almost everything. He thought it was science fiction, but she assured him it was going to work.

At the time, they were in the prototype stage. They were probably at the test stage by now for all he knew. She shouldn't have told him anything about it; he was aware of the regulations. She could lose much more than just her job over something like that, but she was worried. She had told everyone her concerns about what a full-power test might do. No one listened. She wasn't

[25]

Who Owns Tomorrow?

just worried the test might fail. She thought it would be much worse than that. She was worried it would actually work.

Brian turned the corner at silo 16 and saw the weapons officer and COB at the command console for that silo. They were talking to each other, but he was still a little too far away to hear what they were saying.

"Mr. Haskins, what the hell are you doing down here?" Brian asked his weapons officer. "Nothing else to do?"

"Sir," Haskins said, "an odd reading popped up on one of my simulation runs and I thought it best to go to the source for a few tests." He was clearly concerned.

"Okay," Brian said. "What did you find?"

"I don't know," Haskins said. "That's the problem."

Brian looked over at COB. "Well?" He asked.

"I've never seen anything like this, sir," COB said. "If I didn't know any better, I'd think it had been infected by a virus or something. It's just acting odd."

Brian looked back and forth between his weapons officer and COB a couple of times, then at the console.

"A virus?" Brian asked. "What the hell are you talking about?"

"It just seems to be acting odd," Haskins said. "Changing modes on its own, initiating actions that weren't requested, things like that."

"Maybe it's just a bad memory chip or something that's causing the code to be fragmented. Shut it down," Brian said. "We've got three more. All we need for the propellant test is one missile."

He turned and left as Haskins entered the code on the console to shut the silo down.

It took about three minutes to process a normal shutdown of a missile silo, so they waited patiently and watched the display scroll through all the exit stages.

"Does any of this seem familiar to you?" COB asked.

"What are you talking about?" Haskins asked.

"This," COB said. "All of it. The silo in error, you being here, calling the captain down, ... everything. It all seems so familiar."

"You're crazy, COB," Haskins said. "I have no idea what you're ..."

An alarm went off just then, and they both turned to look at the console. It flickered a couple of times, parts of a couple of error messages popped up for a split second, then it went blank.

"Damn," COB said, looking over at Haskins. "This is getting stranger and stranger all the time."

They both left the missile area and Haskins headed back to his station in the control room. He knew exactly what the Chief meant, but he wasn't ready to talk about it yet.

It had taken weeks while Captain Stiles was on his last rotation off the boat for the virus to find someone who would be on the *Tennessee* during its next deployment. It would have taken anyone, it was just blind luck it stumbled on the captain.

Viruses today are so much more sophisticated. The one everyone remembers was the Stuxnet virus developed in 2005 and used in 2010 to disable a quarter of Iran's gas centrifuges in its nuclear program. The virus rapidly changed the centrifuges' rotor speed, setting up vibrations that literally tore the machines apart. That was really the beginning of the smart virus. It had been incredibly well designed and written, not only concerning how effectively it killed its target, but how it actually got in that position in the first place.

This particular virus, the one on Brian's boat, initially infected the cell phone of a base worker who frequented a bar with an unsecured network. He had connected to the network to check his email even though he knew the network was unsecured. He thought he would just jump on, quickly check his email, and then get off. There was a part of the virus that would attach itself to a photo on the phone, just one of the many ways it could move from device to device. He was connected to the network for only 15 minutes, but that's all it took for that small piece of it to download the entire virus onto his phone and go into hiding.

No one on the base ever found out where the virus originated. That was more or less moot now. Once it had infected that cell phone, it just waited. Eventually, that base worker connected his phone to his PC in the crew quarters on base to share photos he had taken on a trip to visit his parents. As soon as the photos were copied to the PC, the virus attached itself to a little-used utility. Then, unknown to anyone, it began scanning the base's network for someone who was on its target list of personnel to be deployed on the *Tennessee*. The first person on the list was Captain Stiles.

It relocated itself onto the captain's PC, imbedded in the same little-used utility, and continued to wait. If it couldn't move to its target media within a fixed number of days, it would have found other crew member's PCs and imbedded itself into as many as it could.

It didn't take long. A week before the rotated-out crew was to go on their next mission, Captain Stiles inserted a USB drive into his PC in his quarters on the base to download a set of his latest orders and updated crew roster. The virus moved itself onto the USB drive and, again, waited. It was just code. What did it know? It would be patient for as long as it took.

The first day on the boat, Captain Stiles plugged the USB drive into his laptop in his quarters on board and the virus moved itself onto that laptop and started to do its real work. It began by scanning the sub's internal network. It split itself into two parts, one that found and infected the first missile silo launch code, and a second that imbedded itself in the sub's communications bus and continued to scan the entire network looking for missile launch control, propulsion and communications. It had sub-routines for each area.

The alarm and screen flicker that COB and Haskins saw were parts of the silo code that had been partially replaced by the virus. Before the silo in error was shut down and went dark, the new subroutine moved itself back out onto the data bus of the sub's communications array and re-joined with the base part of the virus that had taken up residence there. It would most likely take it another hour or two to get itself imbedded in the code in the next silo down the line. It was patient.

Who Owns Tomorrow?

"Captain has the Conn," the XO, Lt. Wade Garrison, said as Brian stepped into the control room. Garrison stepped over to the station just behind the helmsman.

Brian picked up the mic, set it to Sonar and held it in front of his mouth for a few seconds. He intended to check with Sonar, but just stood there and looked around the control room with the strangest look on his face. Garrison saw this, wrinkled his brow and tilted his head at the captain as if to say *what's up*?

Brian shook his head at Garrison, keyed the mic and said, "Sonar, Conn, report all contacts."

A few moments of silence.

"Conn, Sonar, no contacts out to 10,000 meters."

Brian turned around to face the helmsman.

"Helm, bring us to periscope depth," he said.

"Aye, sir, periscope depth," Garrison repeated. "Ten degree up bubble and slow to one third," he said to the helmsman. They busied themselves with the new task, and Garrison stepped over to Brian and whispered just loud enough for him to hear.

"What was that? You okay?"

"I don't know," Brian replied, shaking his head. "We've been here before."

"I know we have," Garrison said. "Last summer we did the same run down the coast."

"No, that's not what I mean. I mean this. This exact set of circumstances, in this precise order."

Garrison looked around the control room and then back at the Captain.

"Meet me in the officer's mess," he whispered. He turned and stepped back to the helmsman station.

"COB, take over the Helm," Garrison said and left the control room.

"Mr. Randall, you have the Conn," Brian said, turning the control room over to the communications officer, Lt. Randall. "I'll be in the officer's mess for a few minutes. Let me know when we get to periscope depth."

"I have the Conn, aye, sir," Randall said as he stepped to the middle of the control room. The Captain left and headed for the officer's mess.

Who Owns Tomorrow?

"What the hell is going on, Captain?" Garrison asked.

"I have no idea, but something is. Get the weapons officer up here."

Garrison made the call, and he and Brian sat in the mess just drinking coffee until the weapons officer joined them.

Haskins stepped into the mess and just looked back and forth between the captain and Lt. Garrison.

"What's up?" he asked as he poured coffee and sat.

Brian just looked at his two most-senior officers.

"I want to know how bad this déjà vu thing is on my boat," he said. "Mr. Haskins, I saw the way you and COB exchanged looks down on Ballistic Row, what the hell's going on?"

"Sir ... Brian, something is going on, but that's not what the looks were about. I think COB feels the same way about the déjà vu we're seeing. But there was something else."

"The déjà vu first," Brian said, his voice softening a bit. "Garrison, if COB, my weapons officer, and I all think there's something going on here, are you going to tell me my XO hasn't felt it too?"

"No, I've felt it," Garrison said. "I just hadn't said anything about it yet. Several crew members have the same feeling, to one degree or another. I have no explanation and have no idea what it is. But it is getting worse. The longer it goes on, the more detailed the feelings become."

"Mass hysteria brought on by some chemical agent or something?" the captain asked.

"Possible," the XO said. "But I doubt it. This is way too specific. If it were induced by something, a chemical agent or something else, I would think it would be a more general feeling. Some crew members, and I gather you two also, have it down to almost daily events now taking place on the sub. That's at a level I've never seen before."

"I agree," Haskins said. "There's something going on here that doesn't make much sense. So much of what's happening on a daily basis seems like it's happened before. So much so, that it's really spooking some of the crew."

"Well," Brian said, "we're not calling this in just yet. They'll think the whole crew, us included, have gone crazy. I don't want to do that unless it becomes absolutely necessary. Now, what's the something else?"

"Sir, … COB thinks, and I agree with him, that there's a bug on the boat," Haskins said.

Brian looked at his XO then said to Haskins, "What do you mean by a bug?"

"A virus. His guess is it came in with one of the maintenance transmissions before we left base or was carried in by someone who didn't know they had it, but that's just speculation. With the current state of virus technology, it could have come in from several sources."

"How is that possible?" The XO asked. "I mean I can see how something could be attached to a maintenance transmission, but how would it get from the central bus to a missile silo?"

"Every piece of code, everywhere, not just on this sub, has an area in itself where another piece of code can hide. It might be a patch area, someplace that's reserved for the people who maintain it to store patches until they get an actual update done. It is possible to write a virus that might move from program to program, using those patch areas, and clear itself in the program it came from."

"So," the captain asked, "it could jump from program to program looking for what it wanted to infect?"

"Yes, that's the idea. I think it's target is a missile silo, based on what COB and I saw it do when we shut down the one that wasn't working quite right."

"But if it jumps around from program to program, how do you stop it from infecting another one? How do you find it?"

"That's going to be the challenge," Haskins said. "And the bigger question is, what's its end goal? Is it just starting at the end of the silo farm and working its way forward to find a live candle or was the first one a fluke?"

"So, it could find a live warhead on its next jump, and if it does, we're all screwed?" the XO asked.

"Not just us," Brian said. "If it finds a live one, we can only assume it is not going to splash it into the Atlantic. It's going to aim it somewhere."

"Yes," Haskins said. "That's the real problem."

"Whether we all have déjà vu or not," the XO said.

"I've got to call this in," Brian said. He looked at his XO. "Get back to the control room and surface the boat, I've got some calls to make." Then he turned to Haskins. "See if you can figure out where it is and a way to stop it. If not, we'll have to pull the plug on the entire boat to stop it. This thing may not even know we're carrying duds in some of the silos, that may be our only saving grace."

Who Owns Tomorrow?

Chapter 3
Event minus 20 hours
DARPA Headquarters, Project Achilles

Karen wasn't able to get out of the house until 10:30 that morning. It took that long to get all the recordings packed away to send to the lab and to hang around long enough to make sure there weren't going to be any more unusual incidents.

All she could do while they were packing up was pace back and forth and talk to Sebastian. He never did say anything back to her.

The support teams left the recording equipment set up just to make sure, and Karen got on the road to the office. Dr. Sheffield followed her in his car. He would be her shadow for the foreseeable future as this case developed. He didn't give her a choice; it was company protocol.

Sebastian was on the front seat next to her, just watching the scenery go by. She wasn't about to leave him behind, not knowing how all this was going to work out. Besides, as she was walking out the door just to load the car, he ran out ahead of her and waited by the passenger door, almost as if he was supposed to go with her today. Strangest thing she had ever seen. He had never done that before.

She couldn't believe what she had heard that morning as the face in the mirror continued to speak, and still couldn't believe who that face belonged to. Dr.

[38]

Sheffield and the rest of the ER crew didn't seem to be perplexed by any of it. They seemed to take it in stride that the person in the mirror was their own Karen Stiles. She ran over it all again in her mind as she made her way through the light traffic into the office.

Who Owns Tomorrow?

"Karen," the face in the mirror said.

"Colonel Karen Stiles," it said.

"We can't see or hear you, but you should be able to see and hear us, my tech people tell me we are in the correct space and time. Please listen carefully. What I'm about to tell you could very well save the world. If you're not already doing so, please record everything. We don't have much time and I will not be repeating any of this message. We only have enough power for a few minutes of this transmission. If we get cut off there may be other messages, but I can't guarantee it.

"This is about the Project Achilles test you have scheduled. I am you, I am Colonel Karen Stiles. I know it's hard to believe, but you must listen to me. You must not …". The transmission went dead and the face and voice disappeared.

They waited almost a full hour for it to start again, but it never came back. A couple of the people sitting in the foyer, none of them familiar to Karen, at once jumped to the conclusion that the voice had meant for them not to do the Project Achilles test. She had to admit that was the most logical conclusion, but no one could be sure. Dr. Sheffield said he would wait until he had a chance to review the entire tape again before drawing any conclusions. She wasn't sure what else he would see. She just thought he was postponing his opinion until they were in the office.

It was obvious it was her image on the mirror, and her voice. She wasn't sure where the person in the mirror was, but she was wearing the same clothes Karen currently had on. It had to be her, and wherever, or whenever, it was, it was soon and close.

Sebastian began to purr and she reached over to pet him. That always seemed to calm them both down.

Who Owns Tomorrow?

Karen walked into the STO and headed toward her office at the back of the floor with her briefcase in one hand and Sebastian in the other. She could feel everyone's eyes on her as she made her way through the maze of the desks on the floor. When she got to her secretary's desk to pick up her messages, Jan just eyed her sideways.

"I heard what happened this morning," Jan said. "What do you think it was?"

"It looks like everyone has heard about it," Karen said as she looked out over the desks on the floor.

"Yeah," Jan said. "Word gets around fast." She tilted her head toward Karen's closed office door, "General Scott is waiting for you."

"Great," Karen said, as she leafed through her messages, trying not to drop Sebastian. "Call me in 15 minutes if he's not out by then."

"Want me to take him off your hands?" Jan pointed to Sebastian.

Karen just smiled and said, "No, the general likes him."

She walked into her office, set the briefcase down on her desk and turned to face General Scott.

"Mark," she nodded. "I'm sure you've heard." Brigadier General Mark Scott was over her area and a couple of others. They were good friends and had known each other since college. He had gotten his first star a little faster than she had and they had always laughed about it together. She joked that he had slept his way to the top and Mark didn't argue with her.

Sebastian jumped onto her desk and proceeded to walk right up to General Scott, onto his lap, and look him right in the eye.

"Mauw," he said.

"Damnit, Karen, you know I don't like cats," he said as he brushed the big tom off his lap. Sebastian walked over and jumped up on the window sill; he was just as happy to settle in there and watch the birds.

"Sorry, I keep forgetting," she smiled.

She poured two cups of coffee and handed one to the general. Jan always did a great job of anticipating her.

"I heard about it from the emergency response team leader but I haven't seen the footage yet. Is it conclusive?"

"Conclusive is an understatement. Go look at the footage, they brought it in-house with us, and then we can talk. If it scares you as much as it does me, we have a lot of things to talk about that will potentially affect Achilles. This is certainly something I've never seen before."

"This is the final few hours before the first test," the general said. "Is it that bad?"

Who Owns Tomorrow?

"Yes, it is. Just look at the footage then come right back here," Karen said. "I've never seen anything like it. It has even got Dr. Sheffield spooked, and I didn't think anything spooked him."

"Jesus, Karen," he said. "I don't have to tell you we don't need any interruptions to the Achilles timeline."

"I know, I know," she said. "General, just look at the footage, then we'll talk."

General Scott left Karen's office without touching his coffee and headed to the Emergency Responder area to look at the footage evidence and talk to Dr. Sheffield.

Karen sat behind her desk, unsure about what to do next. It did seem to her that they should at least think about stopping the test tomorrow morning. She still wasn't sure that was the crux of the message, even though they didn't get it all. Hopefully, after General Scott saw the footage and talked with Dr. Sheffield, they could all come to some consensus.

She picked up the phone and dialed an answering service she and Brian kept. She needed to talk to him. They had a message service set up to notify each other if something happened that would cause them to step outside normal channels. Well, something had happened. And it definitely warranted her stepping outside normal channels.

She left him a message, but it might take a while for him to be able to call, so she began to go through the last set of simulations the crews had done last night.

[44]

General Scott walked into Dr. Sheffield's office and sat in the side chair next to his desk. Sheffield was turned around facing the other way, entering data into his computer terminal and didn't hear the general come in.

"Dr. Sheffield?" The general asked.

Sheffield nearly jumped out of his chair.

"Jesus, General," he said. "Don't do that. You nearly gave me a heart attack."

"Sorry, I thought you heard me come in. I need to talk to you about the 911 call this morning from Colonel Stiles residence."

"I was just finishing my report," Sheffield said.

"Can you give me the bottom line?" the general asked.

"If you mean can I tell you exactly what happened, the answer is no. I can tell you what I think happened, but I have no solid scientific data yet to support it."

"Okay, let's start with that," the general said. "What do you think happened.

"Can we have Karen join us? Let's move into my conference room," Sheffield said. Without waiting for the general to respond, he picked up the phone and called Karen. Civilians were like that sometimes. The general didn't like them very much. He needed some of them, but he didn't like them.

Who Owns Tomorrow?

"Karen, this is Dr. Sheffield, can you join the general and me in my conference room for a discussion about what happened at your house?"

"Sure, I'll be right down."

"Can you bring Jan along to take notes?" Sheffield asked.

"Sure, we're on our way."

Sheffield hung up and proceeded into his adjoining conference room without waiting on the general.

"What if I didn't want any of this down on paper?" the general asked as he took a seat in the small conference room. He was obviously a little peeved.

"Then you could have the conversation with someone else," Sheffield said. "We need to make sure we remember exactly how this transpired and what we all thought about it."

They both sat in silence until Karen and Jan came into the room.

Karen sat next to the general and Jan on the other side of the table, at the end where she could see everyone. "Can we begin now?" the general asked.

It was obvious to Karen and Jan that the general was miffed at Sheffield, probably for what the general considered wasting his time.

Just then a technician brought in a report and handed it to Dr. Sheffield.

"Ah," he said. "Just what I was waiting on."

Karen had brought Sebastian with her and he jumped from her arms and ran over to bookcase on the other side of the conference room. He jumped up on top of a stack of books and curled up just like he belonged there. She thought it was odd because he didn't sniff all over looking for a place to sleep like cats normally do. He went straight for that stack of books. Almost like he'd been there before.

"So," Karen said, "do we know what we saw?"

"Yes," Sheffield said. "We saw you, Karen."

"Well, crap," the general snorted. "This is going to be a colossal waste of my time." He started to get up, but Karen put a hand on his arm without even looking in his direction.

"We know it looked like me, Dr. Sheffield, but how can you be so certain it was me?" She asked.

"Two reasons, now," he said, holding up the report the technician brought in. "The first is you were transmitting from this room. Look around and compare it to the video." He turned a monitor screen around and brought up the image that had been in the mirror in Karen's foyer.

"Not many people come into this conference room," Dr. Sheffield continued. "It's attached to my office on one side and my lab on the other."

They all looked at the image and then around the room. Even though the room in the image was a disaster, it was obvious it was the conference room they were in.

[47]

Who Owns Tomorrow?

The table they were sitting at, the paintings on the walls, and the bookcases where Sebastian was curled up were all there, down to the last detail.

"Well," Karen said, "it certainly looks like this room, but that doesn't mean much."

"But there was one other very conclusive clue in the photo," Dr. Sheffield said. "I didn't even see it at first. One of our technicians caught it doing a closeup analysis."

Dr. Sheffield zoomed in as far as he could without the image becoming too distorted to see clearly. There, plain as day, on the back book shelf behind Sheffield, was Sebastian, her big tom. Curled up, sleeping right where he was now.

Karen gasped. She had thought it was a spur-of-the-moment decision to grab Sebastian when she left this morning. She was beginning to think it was more than a coincidence that Sebastian was so insistent about coming with her.

"Okay," General Scott was the first to speak. "I'll give you that this is the room, or a copy of it, but that doesn't mean this wasn't a faked video somehow engineered to be seen somewhere in Karen's house."

"That brings us to the second reason," Dr. Sheffield said holding up the document. "This is the analysis of the mirror in Karen's foyer. There was tachyon particle residue where the video appeared."

"Oh, my God," Karen said and stood up.

"I don't understand," the general said.

"That means," Karen said, "that at some point in the future I transmitted that video from this room into the past. My past. So I could see it this morning."

Who Owns Tomorrow?

Chapter 4
Event minus 20 hours
DARPA Headquarters Project Darkness

There were really only two projects at DARPA that were currently nearing the critical first test stage. Project Achilles, run by Colonel Karen Stiles and Project Darkness, run by two older, senior researchers, Dr. Sanders and Dr. Miller. No one really expected Project Darkness to actually go anywhere, but it was an interesting avenue of research.

It had taken them a year to set up the project, get all the required approvals, and develop the exotic matter they were using. They had been running simulations now for almost six months.

Today, Dr. Sanders was confused. He looked again at the figures from the latest simulation run of their dark matter generator and they still looked all wrong; they hadn't changed. The numbers were way too high for particle creation considering the energy levels that the simulation ran with. This couldn't be right.

"What's wrong?" Dr. Miller asked. He was Dr. Sanders' associate and was looking over Sanders' shoulders at the report.

"This makes no sense to me," he said out loud. "Is this the first simulation that has reported these numbers?"

Miller flipped through several pages on his clipboard, and looked over his notes from the past simulations.

"As far as I can tell," he said, "yes, it is." He looked again at the latest numbers. "Wait, … there's something else. It looks like there's a faster chain reaction going on in this simulation. This may be what we've been looking for all along. This may be the right frequency."

"Oh, my God," Sanders said. "I think you're right. Have we ever run with this frequency before?"

"Let me look."

Miller went through several layers of reports again on his clipboard.

"Yes, we have, but with other parameters, never in this combination."

"I can't believe we just stumbled onto the right combination so early in the trial process."

They walked into the next room where the dark matter generator was set up. Sanders and Miller were both physicists who had been working for DARPA for the past 30 years. Over the years, they had worked on so many projects they lost count. But they were never the lead on any of the projects. Until now. The new head of the area they were in, General Scott, thought it was about time they got the chance to do whatever they thought might be useful with a new project.

They had designed a neutrino emitter that they were sure would create dark matter particles. Not detect them, but actually create them. Dark matter particles were actually discovered in 2034, but they were still very elusive, so any plan to create them was worth investigating.

The device was in the center of the lab and looked like nothing very important at all. It was on a table about 12 feet square. There was a neutrino emitter bolted to each corner of the table whose only job was to generate streams of high-speed neutrinos. All four of them were aimed at the center of the table where there sat a block of exotic matter whose composition was the subject of at least 12 DARPA patents. Even General Scott was not really sure what was in it. The process was really quite simple, if one believed Sanders and Miller. The high-speed streams of neutrinos would bombard the block of exotic matter and, hopefully, create dark matter particles. There were two dark matter detectors, one on each side of the table, aimed at the block of exotic matter to record the event.

Every simulation they had run so far had yielded no dark matter particles, and both Sanders and Miller were beginning to believe it might take a very long time to find the right combination of variables. Each simulation had the streams of neutrinos vibrating at different frequencies, varying velocities, and various strengths. They were confident the process would eventually work as long as they could find the right combination of strength, velocity, and frequency. Eventually. Maybe they had just found it.

Miller went over to the computer console at one end of the room and began entering commands while Sanders began inspecting the components on the table.

They had never actually run a test yet. Everything had been based on Miller's math and Sanders' design.

The exotic matter was shimmering inside its protective magnetic bubble. It wasn't in the bubble to protect people from it, so they said, but rather to keep it from deteriorating if it was exposed to the atmosphere for any length of time.

"I'm setting things up for another simulation tonight to verify the data we just got," Miller said.

"Good idea," Sanders said. "I'm going to warm everything up and let it stay powered up for a while."

"Just remember to turn everything off before we leave for the evening," Miller said. "That would be quite a waste of power."

"I will, don't worry," Sanders said. They were both very forgetful.

While Miller set up the calculations for the next simulation that evening, Sanders sat at the controls of the remote arm. It was like a high-tech grabber on wheels. He turned it on and maneuvered the arm out to the center of the table to pick up the exotic matter. It had to stay in its magnetic bubble so it didn't deteriorate. This was all they had of this recipe and it had to last. Once he had it in the arm's grasp, he maneuvered the entire apparatus over to the steel cabinet at the other end of the large table.

Who Owns Tomorrow?

He carefully placed the exotic matter on the specially designed platform on the top shelf of the cabinet. It was designed to maintain the magnetic bubble around the matter for several days at a time. He only needed it stored overnight. There were other containers of exotic matter on the same shelf, some from past experiments and some yet to be tried, but all different configurations. The entire shelf was protected by a magnetic field generator.

After he moved the exotic matter, he began turning on all the neutrino emitters to let them warm up for the rest of the day. He and Miller would be back before the end of the day to turn them off.

Chapter 5
Event plus 12 hours
Remains of DARPA Headquarters

Karen was exhausted. Even though it wasn't true, she felt like she hadn't slept in days. It was hard to believe she had been at home a little more than 35 hours earlier, in the suburbs, safe and sound, watching it snow. Her clothes were a mess, she had her hair up in a ponytail, which she never did, and her makeup was long gone.

Sebastian was curled up on a stack of books on one of the only remaining bookcases in the conference room, happily sleeping away. He had been a little concerned when the explosions and fires started, but he found his safe place to hide and that was all that mattered.

Karen and Dr. Sheffield were in Karen's main lab where the shield generator itself was located. They were sitting next to each other at one of the work tables close to the double doors on the north side of the lab that led into the generator room. From where they were, they could see the edge of the shield beyond the generators through the open double doors.

Karen missed Brian. He was probably gone like everyone else. The last time she had talked to him was when his submarine was becoming infected with a virus that was slowly taking over the boat.

She looked at the blackness beyond the shimmer of the Achilles high-energy shield, the only thing that was protecting them. For the moment. It was really actually black beyond the shield. She had no idea what it was, just nothingness perhaps? Maybe they were already inside the rift and just didn't know it. She hung her head and cried. It was really the only thing she could do at the moment.

Dr. Sheffield was sitting next to her and put his arm around her shoulders.

"We'll figure it out," he said. "It'll be okay."

"It'll be okay?" She looked up at him and said through tears. "How can you possibly say that? Everything in the world, except us, is likely gone. Hell, it's probably everything in the entire solar system, maybe even more than that. We just don't know. The only thing keeping us alive is this shield." She got up and moved closer to the shield. She threw her coffee cup at the shimmer, it just bounced off and shattered on the floor. "We don't even know how long the shield will hold out."

Karen hung her head and began to sob again.

"Look," Dr. Sheffield said, "at least the transmission to your past self worked this morning. We know that. The only thing we don't know is if they got the entire message."

"You know damn well they ... we ... didn't. We talked about it already before all this happened, remember?" Karen said. "We were sitting right next door in the conference room with General Scott and Jan." She paused to take a breath and wipe her eyes before she could continue. General Scott and Jan never made it.

"We watched the video that was made in my house, and the transmission was cut off.

"It happened again exactly the same way this morning when we transmitted to the past. Now we know why the transmission suddenly stopped when we saw it in my house. If it hadn't been for Sebastian getting startled and knocking over the tachyon emitter, stopping the transmission, we would have gotten the entire message out."

"We don't know it happened the same way this time," Dr. Sheffield said. "All we can hope is the entire message got through."

"We did this to ourselves trying to play God, you know that," she said, still crying. "This is the most bizarre Hail-Mary pass I've ever seen. How do we even know if we can change the past?"

"We don't," Sheffield said, "but it's the only option we have. In the time we have left."

Karen dried her eyes and walked the rest of the way over to the edge of the shimmering energy field. She reached up and put her hand out to touch the field. It felt a little warm and it pulsed slightly. Project Achilles was at least still protecting them. For how long, no one knew.

"What happens when the generators in this section die?" Karen asked.

"Without power, the field will just go away," Sheffield answered calmly.

Who Owns Tomorrow?

"Just like that," Karen said. "You don't sound too concerned."

"Oh, I am," Sheffield said. "I just think we have priorities, the first being trying to contact the past to see if we can change this, keep it from happening at all."

"And what happens if we do change the past?" she asked, looking at the blackness beyond the shimmer. A rock the size of a house came hurtling out of the darkness and hit the shield. It just bounced off and continued on its way. Karen was so numb from everything that she didn't even flinch.

"If we do change the past, we'll never know," Sheffield said.

"What do you mean?" Karen asked

"Chances are, we'll just cease to exist."

"So, for us it's a no-win situation," Karen said. "If we succeed, we cease to exist and if we fail, everything ceases to exist."

"Yep, that's about the size of it," Sheffield said. "Don't know about you, but I'd rather go out trying to save the world."

"I guess," Karen said. She thought about it for another few minutes. "So you think if the past actually changes things so that the shield is up when the disaster happens, then all this," she swept her arm around, "doesn't happen and we will just vanish as a failed possible future?"

Sheffield thought about it for a few seconds and said, "Yes, I think so."

"Didn't you ever see that old movie called *A Sound of Thunder* made way back in 2005?" Karen asked.

"I don't watch many movies," Sheffield said, "particularly older ones."

"Well, maybe you should," Karen said. "In that movie, the past was changed and it caused what they called *time waves* that rippled through the ages and eventually reached the present. The characters would watch the world change around them based on what was changed in the past. I think that's probably what would happen. We may still be here and we may even remember what it used to be like, it's just the world that would be different."

"I doubt that would actually happen," Sheffield said. "I think it would be more instantaneous and, if we're still here, we would remember nothing about it."

"But you don't really know, do you?" Karen asked.

"No, I don't," Sheffield said. "It's all conjecture."

Karen was quiet for a while. Thinking.

"What about some of the moral implications?" Karen asked.

"Now what are you talking about?"

"Who owns tomorrow?" she asked.

Who Owns Tomorrow?

He stopped what he was doing and looked over at her. "What?"

"Why do we have any right to ask someone in the past to change what they're doing to affect the future? Every little thing they do affects this future for everyone, not just us, all the time. I understand we're trying to save the world, but don't they have the right to make decisions for themselves that affect their future? Why should we have the right to tell them how their future should go?"

"But their future is our present," Sheffield said.

"That's my point exactly," Karen said. "It's their future, not ours. Let me put it this way. How would you feel if you got a message from yourself in the future telling you, not asking you, but telling you to do something you weren't originally going to do?"

"I guess I never really thought about it that way." He grumbled something about damn intellectuals, and went back to entering data on his laptop.

Karen was still quiet, deep in thought. What if we convinced the people in the past to do something that ultimately caused even more damage? Although it was hard to fathom anything worse than what they were now experiencing, it was entirely possible that this was still a relatively local event. What if we convinced them to put the shield up sooner and it stopped this disaster but created another one that was even worse? Did she and Dr. Sheffield really have the right to dictate to the people in the past, regardless of what we might want them to do?

She turned back to Dr. Sheffield. "When is our next window to try to send another message?"

"Four more hours," Sheffield said. "It'll take that long to recharge the tachyon emitters."

Karen came back over to the work table in her central lab area and sat back down. Even though the disaster happened about 12 hours ago, this area of DARPA headquarters was still a shambles. There was smoke and rubble everywhere from the explosions in and around the building and small fires still burned here and there. Some security guards who were in this section when it happened tried to put the fires out whenever they popped up, but it seemed to be never ending. All together, there were only 45 people left in what used to be a thriving research and development outpost with a normal, daily staff of about 2,000.

Perhaps only 45 people left anywhere.

"Do you really think this will work?" She asked Sheffield.

"The theory is sound," he said. "Beyond that, your guess is as good as mine." He turned back his laptop and continued entering commands. "We'll have to change the focus and direction of the beams this time, I think your past self will be in her office when we're ready to try again."

"That should be where she was. Where I was. Where we'll be, ... hell this is so confusing. So you really think you know what will happen if this doesn't work?"

"Yes, the world ends. That's all. What else could there be?"

"Is that it, really?" she asked. Sheffield didn't answer. He was deep in the calculations to pinpoint their exact location in the grand scheme of the universe hours ago so he could aim the tachyon emitters where Karen used to be. But he had an idea that it wasn't the end. He thought this bizarre tale would go on and on, but he didn't even want to bring it up right now. Things were just too chaotic. Everyone at any point in their timeline has a past, no matter how far back you go.

The thought that Karen had done all this before still nagged at her and got stronger all the time. This was the first time she wondered how many times they had done this? It just didn't make any sense.

Karen got up and went back to the edge of the shield. She tried to pin down that nagging thought about all of this happening before. Was it actually a memory or just wishful thinking? Was this a local event whose boundaries they just couldn't see or was it something larger? Perhaps even the end of everything?

She put her hand back up on the shield and felt it's warmth. All she saw was blackness and a faint flicker off in the distance every once in a while. She had no idea what that was or how far away it was. It could have been halfway to the moon for all she knew.

What if Dr. Sheffield was right? Even if they did convince the past to do something different, how did they know this wasn't the first time all this had happened? If everyone, and everything, just vanished if the past was changed, they wouldn't now know they had done this before. It was all so confusing.

Did she do this herself? Did she cause this disaster by delaying the shield? If she had just left things alone, at least this future wouldn't have happened. But what would have?

She when back through her central lab into Dr. Sheffield's conference room where Sebastian was comfortably sleeping on his stack of books. She

Who Owns Tomorrow?

scratched him between the ears and he opened his eyes
and looked up at her.

What did he know that no one else did? Or was
this all just her imagination, too?

He tilted his head to the side and rubbed his face
on her hand.

"Meow," he said, softly. He looked back up at her
and started purring. She looked into his eyes and saw
nothing but a sleepy cat.

Chapter 6

Event minus 15 hours

DARPA Headquarters Project Achilles

"Just as I thought," the general said again as he looked up at Karen standing next to him. "Now I know this is wasting my time."

He began to move in his seat indicating he was about to stand up as Dr. Sheffield shook his head and said, "Damn it, general, get your head out of your ass and look around. This is the room in the video!"

Karen put her hand on his shoulder and said, "Mark, this is real. That residue can only mean someone was trying to communicate with the past."

"Aren't we getting a little out into the weeds of science fiction talking about communicating with the past? The past has already happened." He turned the video screen toward him and surveyed it as he looked around the room. Everything was the same. Everything except the rubble. The cat was even sitting in the same spot.

"It depends on which interpretation of time that you subscribe to and how it flows," Sheffield said. "It in fact may be possible to send a message back in time. Actually traveling to the past is another story altogether, but sending a message back to the past may be possible."

"Humor me," the general said. "Pretend I don't know anything about physics."

Who Owns Tomorrow?

"It was thought that tachyon particles could actually travel faster than the speed of light and might be used to beam something into the past, usually a message," Karen said.

"She is correct," Sheffield said, "We've been loosely playing with it here for a couple of years. What did you think we were doing here?"

"I thought it was all just research," the general said. "You mean you had successfully communicated with the past prior to this? Why wasn't I told? This could be the biggest breakthrough in military history."

"I said loosely playing with it, General," Sheffield said. "Actually communicating with the past, sending a message, has other implications I wasn't ready to commit to yet. All we can do now is send a traceable tachyon pulse a day or so into the past."

"Well, if what you're telling me here today is true, you have already figured it out," the general said. "Or you will. You both just said that the transmission recorded in Karen's residence this morning was broadcast from here sometime in the future. Sometime soon. Correct?"

Karen just looked at Dr. Sheffield and said, "Well?"

Dr. Sheffield got up from his desk and walked around the conference room for a few seconds with his hands in his pockets, mumbling to himself.

"Okay, okay," he said, sitting back down, "yes. I have some ideas about how it could work, but I've never tested them."

"Well, apparently they work," the general said. "Congratulations. Now what do we do? Doesn't this seem to indicate that something will happen, shortly, that causes us to take the unimaginable step of trying to contact the past to undo it?"

"Yes, I would think so," Karen said. "The only question is, what?"

"Come on guys, I'm not the sharpest pencil in the box but even I can figure this one out. I would suspect," the general said, glancing at Karen, "that since it was you trying to contact your past self, and I can't believe I just said that, it means it has something to do with your project test coming up. Don't you think?"

"You did say 'you must not …' in the recording," Sheffield said. "I think it's pretty clear what that meant."

"Not necessarily," Karen said. "I now believe the transmission was inconclusive as far as I'm concerned. She … I … could have just as easily have said 'you must not delay the test you're about to do.' Absent other communications, I don't think we can say one way or another what she meant."

"You know," the general said, "yours is the only major project scheduled for a test tomorrow morning."

"Yes, I am aware of that," she said. "I still think we should go ahead. You of all people should agree with me, you know what this project could mean for the military."

"How long a delay are we talking about if we miss this test?" he asked.

"The biggest problem is the very real possibility of the fuel we're using for the initial shield startup going bad and perhaps not being able to get more of the main ingredients quickly. It has an incredibly short half-life. There are so many projects like mine that use some of the same ingredients, it could cost us a long delay," Karen said. "It could mean days or weeks, even a couple of months."

"I can't help that," the general said. "Dr. Sheffield, what do you think?"

"I'm generally inclined to agree with Karen, but I do worry about the possibility that we're wrong."

"Explain," the general said.

"Well, look at it from it from a purely logical standpoint. I mean, let's face it, if they really wanted us to go ahead with the test, why contact us at all? They, we, knew that was what we were going to do in any case, so why go to the trouble of trying to send a message back into the past? The only reason would be to stop the test."

"Interesting thought," the general said. "Unless, of course, we knew they were thinking that anyway and we just wanted to be sure."

"That might imply that something else happens that causes us to reconsider everything," Dr. Sheffield said.

"I don't know," Karen said. "I think this is all idle speculation and we should proceed with what we know is sound science. The message was incomplete and therefore inconclusive. We need to proceed as we would normally unless and until we get more information."

"I may not like it," the general said, nodding toward Karen, "but the decision is yours."

"Good," Karen said. "In that case, we'll go ahead with the test on schedule."

"I hope she knows what she's doing," Dr. Sheffield said after Karen had left the room.

"I hope you both know what you're doing," the general said as he left.

Dr. Sheffield sat at his conference table and tapped his pen absently on his notebook. He had a thought about how to send a message back in time. He got up and headed into his lab.

Who Owns Tomorrow?

Brian went back to his quarters and grabbed his satellite phone. After he talked to Command he needed to call Karen. There were things going on that she needed to know. If his sub was infected with some kind of virus, it may affect DARPA.

"Captain has the Conn," the XO said as Brian got back to the control room. The sub was just about to surface.

"Sonar, Conn," Brian said into the mic. "Report all contacts."

"Conn, Sonar, two Russian destroyers, one on either side. Look to be Udaloy class, about 2,000 meters out."

"Helm, all stop, zero bubble," Brian shouted to the helmsman.

"All stop, aye, sir," the XO repeated. "Helm, all stop, zero bubble."

Brian walked over to the Sonar station and looked at the screens as the sub started to level off.

"What's going on? Why weren't these reported as soon as you saw them?"

"Sir," the sonar operator said, "they were. They just appeared out of nowhere when you called for all contacts. I can't explain it, but there they are."

As they both watched the sonar screens, both destroyers maneuvered a little north and south and then disappeared right before their eyes. One moment, they were big as life on the sonar screens, the next they were gone.

The sonar operator scrambled and readjusted all the instruments.

"Nothing," he said, looking up at the captain. "They're gone. You saw them, didn't you?"

"Yes, I saw them," the captain said. "Helm, surface," he called over his shoulder.

"Aye, surface," the XO said. He turned to the Helm and said "10 degree up-bubble, engines to one third, up slow and steady."

"XO on me," Brian said as he moved to the tower ladder. "Lt. Randall, you have the Conn." They both waited there as the pumps emptied the bridge once the sub was on the surface. When the green light came on, they opened the hatch and proceeded up.

There was no surface traffic as far as the eye could see. Not only no Russian destroyers, but nothing.

"Dammit, Garrison," Brian said. "What the hell is going on here? Sonar clearly reported two Russian destroyers close enough to spit on, and then they disappeared."

Who Owns Tomorrow?

The XO just scanned the horizon while Brian picked up the inter-ship mic.

"Radio, Bridge, get me COMSUBLANT," Brian said.

"Bridge, Radio, aye, sir."

"Brian, I don't see anything, all the way out to the horizon," the XO said. "You think this is more virus fallout?"

"It has to be."

"Bridge, Radio," the voice on the mic returned. "Sir, I can't raise Atlantic Command. Everything seems to be working on our end, but I get nothing but static."

"Radio, Bridge, wait one."

Brian just looked at his XO. "Wade, when was the last time we couldn't raise Atlantic Command?"

"Well," the XO said, "Ummm, never that I know of."

"Exactly," Brian said. "Something's going on and I don't like it one bit."

"Try the Pacific side, the satellite should relay it from here," Garrison said.

Brian nodded as he keyed the mic. "Radio, Bridge, try COMSUBPAC."

"Bridge, Radio, aye, sir."

"Good idea," Brian said. "Let's hope it's just a fluke."

"Bridge, Radio," the reply came, "I can't raise them either. I re-checked the equipment and it's not on this end."

Brian turned around and looked at the antenna array just outside the conning tower. Nothing looked damaged; it all looked fine.

"Radio, Bridge, get up here and check out all the antennas. I'm going to try the sat phone."

"Bridge, Radio, aye, sir."

Brian keyed in Karen's office number, screw protocol. Something was going on and maybe she could shed some light on it. At any rate, she needed to know about the virus, just in case it was more pervasive than just his sub.

"Colonel Stiles office, can I help you?" Jan said.

"Jan, this is Brian on the sat phone, is Karen around?"

"Hold on, she just walked back in."

Brian waited while Jan got Karen on the phone. He still wasn't sure what he should tell her.

"Brian," Karen said when she got to the phone, "did you get my message?"

"No," he sounded surprised. "That's not why I'm calling. What happened?"

"It's hard to explain," she said. "We've just had strange things happening here since this morning."

Who Owns Tomorrow?

"Same thing here," Brian said. "That's why I'm calling. Not sure if what's happening here will affect you or not, but you need to know."

"I'll bet you even money what happened here isn't what's happening on your boat," Karen said. "You first."

"We have what we believe may be a virus corrupting parts of the sub's processing, potentially including the missile silos. Your turn."

"We believe that my future self contacted me this morning at the house," Karen said

There was a pause for a few seconds.

"Okay, you win, I can't top that. What the hell are you talking about?"

"It's very complicated," Karen said, "but it appears that my future self, tomorrow morning sometime to be exact, sent me, will send me, a message back in time."

"What did the message say?" Brian asked. He had learned a long time ago to never doubt anything that happened at DARPA.

"That's part of the problem," Karen said. "The message got cut off. All it said was, 'You must not ...'. That was it."

"What do you think your future self was talking about?"

"Well," she said, "everyone's assuming it has something to do with the test we are planning on running on the energy shield."

"Do you think you were trying to warn yourself not to do the test?"

"That's the immediate thought, but I think I have everyone calmed down. As pointed as that warning was, I still think it's inconclusive. Just like an incomplete EAM in your line of work. It must be ignored until a more complete message arrives."

"Well," Brian said, "I don't know if what I have to tell you will change your mind or not, but it's certainly causing us grief."

"How bad is it?"

"It first popped up in one of the missile silos, and now I think it has moved into the communications array. We can't raise either sub Command, the Atlantic or Pacific. I'm worried about what's next."

"Do you think this virus is more pervasive than just on your boat?" Karen asked.

"That's why I called," Brian said. "I think you might want to consider that anything out of the ordinary that's happening could be part of the same attack, if that's what this is. We haven't identified the virus yet, but it could have come from only a handful of places. If the purpose of this thing is to try to launch a missile, it's in the right place and has already been in one of the silos."

"If a virus like that gets into DARPA," Karen said, "it could do more damage than what could be caused by the missiles on your sub. This puts a new perspective on everything. We may want to consider shutting everything down until we can do a sweep of the entire facility to make sure we're not infected as well."

Horns started blaring and Brian and the XO could tell that the boat had started to submerge.

"What's happening?" Karen asked.

"The boat has started to dive on its own, as far as I can tell from where I am. I may not be able to talk again until we can get control of the boat. Stay safe and do what you need to," Brian said. Karen hadn't heard any of it as the call had already been disconnected.

"Helm, Bridge, what the hell is happening down there?"

"Bridge, Helm, not sure, sir, but you'd better get down here. The boat is diving and we can't get control. The hatch controls aren't even working, unless you get down here and manually close the hatch, the boat's going to be flooded."

Brian and Wade and the radio operator who was looking at the antennas scrambled down the ladder and secured both hatches just as the boat slipped beneath the water. Brian and the XO went to the Helm.

"We have no control of the bow planes, the rudder or the engines. The boat seems to be headed down and I have no idea when it's going to stop," Lt. Randall said.

"Mr. Haskins," Brian said, "have you found anything yet?"

Haskins was at the communications control station in the control room, working three different screens.

"Yes, and no, sir," he said. "You'd better look at this."

Brian looked over his weapons officer's shoulder at the center screen.

"I think I've found the bug," Haskins said. "Or at least part of it. Look at this." He pointed to the center screen. The screen was full of numbers in neat rows, except right at the bottom there was an obvious date and some other letters. "This is a dump of part of the missile silo code, it's been overwritten by virus code I can't make heads or tails of, and at the bottom of it is a footprint of sorts."

"Lee," Brian yelled to the other side of the control room, "over here, please."

Petty Officer First Class Thomas Lee rounded the periscope tubes from his station at Combat Control to Communications Control.

"Lee, is this Chinese or Korean or something else?" Brian asked.

Lee leaned in close to the screen and said, "Sir, it's Korean. What you're looking at is called an eye-catcher in coding circles. It's the signature of a cyber group that has been active in North Korea for the last couple of years. They always sign their work with this. They are the group whose virus code brought down that 777 last year over New York. The group has never been found and their viruses always work. If that's really what this is, we're screwed."

"Is there any way to tell what the code is actually doing?" Brian asked. "Can you read the code itself?"

"I can usually read most virus code, given enough time," Lee responded, "but this is different. They do something no one else does to protect their code. The code itself is encrypted by an engine they developed. No one else knows anything about the encryption engine, except that it doesn't decrypt the code until just before it releases it to whatever its target is. So, what you're looking at here is gobbledygook without knowing how that encryption engine works. And we don't even know if this code has been deployed yet, or not. This could be the original code and it's already been decrypted and deployed and we just don't know where."

"So where does that leave us?" Brian asked.

"Essentially," Lee said, "you don't know where it's going to hit until something happens."

"You mean like the propulsion systems being out of our control?" Haskins asked to no one in particular.

Lee went back to his station and the control room got very quiet.

"Helm, where are we?" Brian called out.

"Sir, we are approaching launch depth and slowing to a crawl," Garrison said.

"Do you think that's what the virus is trying to do? Launch?" Brian asked.

"It sure looks like it, sir," Haskins said. "Silo 15 is tuning up for a pre-launch check. It looks like the virus moved from tube 16 down the line to the next missile."

"Can you shut that tube down from up here?" Brian asked. "It seemed to take it a while to go from 16 to 15, if we can kill it here, maybe that buys us some time."

"At the stage it's in now, I would have to actually pull the power from silo control at the missile bay," Haskins said.

"Then go, go," Brian replied. "COB, go with him."

The two took off as Brian searched his mind for a possible solution. They had to get to the surface, that was all there was to it. He couldn't attempt the solution he thought of under water, it was too dangerous.

"Lee, if we shut everything down, I mean a full power down, when we come back up will the virus still be there?"

"It depends, sir," Lee said. "If whatever the virus initially loaded from is not on or up any more, then yes, it might work. Otherwise, it'll just reload and start over."

"But even at that, it will buy us some additional time to try to stop it. Yes?"

"Yes, that is correct, sir." Lee said.

Brian picked up the mic. "Weapons Officer, Conn. Haskins, are you there yet?"

"Yes, sir, we're here. I'm attempting to power down silo 15. Wait one."

Event minus 8 hours
DARPA Headquarters Project Achilles

"Brian! Brian, are you still there?" Karen waited for another few minutes before she disconnected the call on her end. She knew what the alarms she heard over the Sat phone were. The sub was diving and it didn't sound like they had configured it to dive. That meant the virus was in control of the propulsion systems of the boat.

This was not good news. She pressed the intercom for Jan.

"Yes, Colonel"

"Have General Scott and Dr. Sheffield come up to my office right away. This is a must-meet, I don't care where they are, they both need to be here."

"Yes, ma'am, I'm on it," Jan said.

Karen walked over to the bookshelf where she kept her office bar and poured a short scotch. Now, just a few hours after convincing her leadership that she needed to go ahead with the test coming up shortly, she had to convince them she was wrong and they needed to be cautious and even shut down sections to scan for a new virus. Not her favorite thing to do.

"Well, this doesn't look good," General Scott said as he came in and sat in front of Karen's desk. Karen brought him a scotch while they waited on Dr. Sheffield.

[81]

"No, it's not good," Karen said. "In fact, it's much worse than we thought."

Just then, Dr. Sheffield came in and sat next to the general. "What's worse than we thought?" he asked.

"Generally, everything," Karen said. "Doctor, a drink? Help yourself," Karen pointed to the bar on the far wall.

"Well, now I know it's bad," Dr. Sheffield said. "If we're starting to drink this early …"

"I talked to Brian," Karen said to General Scott after downing her scotch and heading over to the bar for another.

"I thought he was currently deployed?" the general asked.

"Who's Brian?" Sheffield asked.

"Brian is my husband," Karen said. "Captain Brian Stiles of the U.S.S. *Tennessee.*"

"The currently deployed captain of a nuclear ballistic submarine," the general said, looking at Karen.

"Oh," Sheffield said. "I would suppose that's an issue somehow."

"Yes, it is," the general said.

"It couldn't be helped," Karen said. "For one thing, he called me. And once you hear what he had to say, you might change your tune."

"I'm listening," the general said.

Karen related Brian's story about the virus to the general and Dr. Sheffield. Paying particular attention to the part about the virus starting in one of the missile silos, then moving into the communications array to stifle communication, and finally, just Karen's speculation based on the alarms she heard at the end of the call, it had control of the boat.

"It sounded to me like they were losing control of the helm while I was talking to them," Karen said. "That means there's a virus in a missile silo on a nuclear ballistic submarine they can't control. Off the coast of DC somewhere," she pointed out the window.

"Exactly where were they?" General Scott asked.

"We didn't discuss that, he probably wouldn't have told me even if I had asked," Karen said.

"And I assume we don't have any way to call him back?"

"Not directly. We share an answering service for messages and he has a satellite phone. But, assuming they're having trouble getting control of propulsion and communications, they may not even be on the surface."

"I need to make a call," General Scott said, and left the room.

"Do you think there's a possibility that the virus is in more places than that submarine?" Sheffield asked.

"I don't think we can take the chance that it's not," Karen said. "Do you?"

"No, I don't. I also don't think that has anything to do with our issue of you trying to contact yourself from the future. Do you?"

Who Owns Tomorrow?

"I can't see how the two could possibly be related, except that now the virus is making us reconsider our decision to go ahead with the test in a few hours," Karen said.

"How so?" Sheffield asked.

"Well, if there's even a remote possibility that this facility might come under the a similar attack, think of the damage. The only way to mitigate that possibility is to do a shutdown of all systems, a virus sweep, then bring everything back up."

"That takes a while," Sheffield said.

"Yes, it does."

"Well, I have some additional information," General Scott said as he stepped back in the room. "I have contacted Atlantic Command directly and they are now aware of the situation. According to them, the U.S.S. *Tennessee* is on a special run. Four of its missiles are duds to test a new solid fuel in actual launch conditions. The plan is to run down the coast and launch one of then just south of DC, just south of here, in fact. If the virus has infected that boat intending to fire a missile, it may not know about the duds."

"Then it makes sense what the virus is doing," Karen said. "Taking control of the missile silos, yes, but also blocking communications and taking over propulsion. It's trying to get to launch depth before the boat can call anyone."

"Atlantic Command is concerned that the virus could get past the four lame birds and happen on a live missile," the general said. "If that happens and it does launch, one missile could take out several of the major cities on the east coast."

Karen knew what was coming. She sat up straighter in her chair waiting for it.

"They have no choice," the general said, "Command has sent two Los Angeles class attack subs after the *Tennessee*. I'm sorry, Karen."

"So, they will destroy the sub and the whole crew while that crew is doing everything they can to stop this?" Karen asked. It was obvious she was angry and agitated. She stood from her desk and walked around the room for a few seconds. She closed her eyes and took two deep breaths. She finally smiled and sat back down and said, "The only saving grace is that they'll never find Brian, he can evade anyone."

"Are we sure there's no way to contact him?" Dr. Sheffield asked.

"Command will try EAMs to see if they get through," the general said, "but if the virus is stopping outbound communications, chances are it's blocking incoming also.

"But we can't worry about that now. Atlantic and Pacific Command are recalling all the subs and every base is going through a lockdown and purge to eliminate any virus. We've got to figure out what to do here to protect ourselves and the projects in case this is more pervasive than just one submarine."

"Karen, if we shut everything down, how long will it take you to power everything back up to make your test?" Dr. Sheffield asked.

"Well, as you know, the shield uses an exotic power supply to initiate, but then it can be maintained with traditional generators. In that sense, it's kinda like a large air conditioner. It takes a lot more power to get it started than it does to keep it running. If we shut down the process of mixing the fuel for the power cells for the shield now," Karen said, "it will take about two or three hours to finish mixing and fueling, and then about another hour to bring everything back up."

Dr. Sheffield glanced at his watch. "By my watch we have about six hours left before the test. If we stop fuel mixing now and shut down all the systems to do a virus check, we still have at the outside a couple of hours left before the test. That sound right?"

"If everything goes well and there are no problems, yes," Karen said. "But that's cutting it pretty thin. The fuel we're using to initiate the test has an extremely short half-life, so if we miss that window we will likely have to start all over."

"I understand," Dr. Sheffield said. "What we should probably do to expedite the process is start with Karen's department. Everything in the building is pretty well compartmentalized, so we can shut things down one project at a time, and do the scans. If it's clean, we bring it back up and move on to the next."

"General?" Karen asked.

"Shut it down."

Who Owns Tomorrow?

Chapter 7
Event minus 5 hours
DARPA Headquarters projects Shutdown - Achilles

Dr. Sheffield sat in his conference room creating a list of the projects that should be shut down and the order in which they should be shut down. He had been in his lab working on his idea about sending messages back into the past when he got called up to Colonel Stiles' office and all the shutdown craziness started. He needed to eventually get back to that work, but this came first.

He had probably the most premium suite of offices and labs in the entire complex. They were almost in the exact center of the DARPA complex, deep inside the largest of the four buildings. The conference room, where he spent most of his time, was between his actual office and his large lab. He used the conference room as his office most of the time because it afforded him the ability to spread out to work.

There was a long hall behind his conference room, to the north, and another long hall in front of it, to the south. Across the hall to the north was Colonel Stiles' main lab complex where her team mixed the shield's initiation fuel and housed the shield apparatus itself. Those labs ran almost the entire length of Dr. Sheffield's lab, conference room, and office. Across the hall to the south was Project Darkness. Dr. Sheffield knew next to nothing about it, so he put it low on his list.

When he finished the list, he got up and went across the north hall to Colonel Stiles' lab complex. He was always amazed at the size and complexity of her lab setup. The room itself was pretty much the size of a basketball court, about three times the size of his lab. At one end, enclosed by hard plexiglass with its own ventilation system, was the shield initiation fuel mixing and storage area. It was a pretty caustic and volatile mix and everyone was in full hazmat suits with respirators.

At the other end were a half dozen eight-foot tables with terminals connected to private servers behind them.

In the center of the lab was the shield initiator itself. There were thick power and control cables running to it from the fuel and server area. Colonel Stiles didn't know this, but Dr. Sheffield had been paying close attention to her work since this project started. He was positive it would work and work well. It looked like a half-sphere, sitting on the floor, surrounded by four columns, each about three feet tall and a foot in diameter. The half-sphere had a five foot radius and was bolted to the floor.

The four columns held the fuel mixture to initiate the shield. It was a blend of deuterium laced with antimatter. Each column was a small, standalone fast-fusion reactor, and combined they had the kick to get the shield up. No radiation to speak of, just a tremendous, quick release of energy.

Who Owns Tomorrow?

The shield would deplete all the fuel in all four reactors in about 30 seconds. It took that long to raise the shield, so to speak. Obviously one of the things that needed to be worked on to make it a viable military asset. In order for it to be useful for military applications, the shield startup time would have to be brought down to, at the outside, a few seconds. Less than a second would be desirable. Once it was up, it could be maintained with simple off-the-shelf high-voltage generators.

"Dr. Sheffield," Karen yelled from across the lab, "over here!"

He made his way through the maze of cables, servers, and terminals to where Karen was. She was checking things off a list on a clipboard and talking to several people in white lab coats.

"I'm just making sure the fuel mixing process gets shut down correctly," Karen said. "We need to start a clock when we shut down the mixing apparatus so we know when it has reached its potency threshold."

"Hopefully, you won't be shut down that long," Dr. Sheffield said. "Are these all the servers we will need to scrub?"

"No," Karen said. "There are about twice that many in the next room," Karen pointed to the lab across the next hall to the north.

"Well, go ahead and do what you need to in order to shut everything down, and let me know when you're ready for the IT teams to come in and do the deep scans."

"I don't like this at all," Karen said. "We're cutting things really close if we need this shield."

"I know," Dr. Sheffield said. "I agree, but it can't be helped right now."

Who Owns Tomorrow?

DARPA Headquarters projects Shutdown - Darkness

Sanders and Miller had gone home with most of the day employees at DARPA and neither one of them had remembered to shut down the neutrino emitters in their lab.

Even though they were on the same extended team led by General Scott, they had no idea what was going on with any of the other projects. They weren't even aware of what most of the other projects were.

To say their experiment was warmed up and ready to go by the time they left for the day was an understatement. The emitters were so warm they created a shimmering effect above and around them. They would even be hot to the touch and were beginning to emit an almost imperceptible low whine. With the frenzy going on with Project Achilles, no one would even be walking down the hallway outside the Project Darkness lab, let alone hear anything inside.

The exotic matter was locked away in the cabinet at the end of the large table that housed the emitters. It's a funny thing about exotic matter. It's called exotic, but it really should be called *unknown*. Not that its ingredients are unknown. There are patents proclaiming that it is composed of 20 percent this and 30 percent that, all on file with the patent office. No, that's not the problem.

The real problem with exotic, aka unknown, matter is no one knows how it will react in any given circumstance. No one. Hell, no one even really knows how it works in the first place. One can run as many simulations as one possibly can, develop as many theories as can be thought of, and trust in as many hopes and aspirations as the next guy, but when the real experiment actually starts, all bets are off. They used to say the best battle plan in the world always goes out the window on the first day of the conflict. This is even worse. It takes less than a second to see what will really happen when you throw the power switch on an experiment like this, and sometimes even that's way too long.

Fifteen years ago, in 2025, an exotic matter experiment on a deserted island owned by the U.S. went terribly wrong. The lead researcher was essentially trying to do the same thing Sanders and Miller are now trying, with only slight differences.

He threw the power switch himself in a televised ceremony. Bad move. If he was still alive to tell you, he would probably say, "All I saw was a light as bright as the sun and then nothing." He and the rest of the research team and their families and all the myriad support personnel, somewhere around 1,000 people on the island, went out like the proverbial light. The island itself

Who Owns Tomorrow?

disappeared meters below the water line, vaporized by the energy release, and nothing was ever found that could explain what went wrong. The lead researcher was working on his own, not affiliated with any major organization, self-funded, and he had no other notes other than what he had with him at the time of the experiment.

Needless to say, it didn't go as planned and they still don't really know what the problem was. Upper management at DARPA was keenly aware of that episode and the thought was that if Project Achilles was a success, the shield would be used to cover the entire Project Darkness experiment when it was tested, just in case. If Achilles didn't work, they were willing to scrap Project Darkness no matter what.

Chapter 8
Event minus 4 hours
U.S.S. *Tennessee*

Brian waited patiently for his weapons officer to get back to him. Externally. Internally he was pacing back and forth, drumming his fingers on everything he touched, and muttering to himself about how long everything took.

"Conn, Haskins," came over the radio. "We got silo 15 down."

"Haskins, Conn, was it a controlled shutdown, or did you just pull the plug, so to speak?"

"Conn, Haskins, we just pulled the plug," Haskins said. "And it's not that easy to do, whether you like it or not, it involved a hatchet and both of us almost getting electrocuted."

"Haskins, Conn, good job, men, I'm glad you're okay. Now, get back up here, we still have work to do." He turned to the Petty Officer Lee at Combat Control, "What do you think, Lee?"

"Sir, that's an even better shutdown for the missile silos. Going down like that means it may take longer now for the core virus to notice the silo component is no longer communicating with it."

"Good. Helm, are we still locked up?"

"Aye, sir, still no control."

"Okay, everyone, hang on, let's bring this thing to the surface manually." Haskins and COB had just walked into the control room. "Haskins, you and COB get ready with Petty Officer Lee's help to shut down the critical components once we break the surface. We can't try this while we're submerged, there's always the chance we can't get anything back up." Brian stepped back to the center of the control room. "Helm, emergency blow!!"

The helmsman stood up and grabbed both chicken switches and pulled them both up, manually blowing compressed air from the storage tanks into the main ballast tanks. Immediately, the boat lost several million pounds of water ballast and the front of the boat tilted up and began to surface quickly.

"She's trying to fight it, sir," the helmsman said, "but I don't think it can stop the surface. All the ballast valves have opened and the tanks are filling again, but it's too late, we're almost on the surface. Our momentum will carry us the rest of the way."

"Haskins, Lee, COB, ... get ready," Brian said.

Haskins was on the propulsion control circuits, COB was on the communications circuits, and Lee on combat control, which included missile control. Unfortunately, but most of the time fortunately, there was no such thing as a single electrical cutoff for everything on a submarine. Single points of failure were avoided in most cases.

The sub broke the surface and Brian yelled, "Now!"

COB, Haskins, and Lee all shut down their respective stations at the same time. Lee could do the combat control circuits from his main panel, but Haskins and COB had to get flat on their backs to pull the plug for communications and propulsion. In a matter of seconds the control room got a lot quieter and a lot darker.

"Don't restart anything yet, open the hatches," Brian said. "COB, join me up top," Brian said as he moved to the main hatch. "Everyone on local, offline walkies."

COB and Brian went up to the Bridge with high-powered binoculars. COB began scanning the horizon as Brian talked to the control room.

"Sonar, Bridge, report all contacts."

"Bridge, Sonar, clear out to 10,000 meters. That's all the range I can get in these waters while we're on the surface."

"Conn, Bridge, start to bring everything up and report as things happen."

"Bridge, Conn, aye, sir," Haskins said.

"Propulsion coming back on line," Haskins said over the walkie. "It seems like we have helm control so far."

"Bridge, Sonar, two contacts just breaking 9,500 meters, both on our port side. Their profile suggests Los Angeles attack class and from the sound of their screws, they're ours. Sir, they are our own subs!"

Who Owns Tomorrow?

"Conn, Bridge, is communications all the way back up yet?"

Haskins looked over at the radio operator and he just shook his head, "Probably another five minutes."

"Bridge, conn, another five minutes," Haskins said.

"That's too long," Brian said out loud to himself. "You see anything, COB?"

"No, they're still too far out to see with these," COB said. "But, they are ours, right? Why worry about them, maybe they can help."

"Sonar, Bridge, can you tell if they know we're here or not?"

"Bridge, Sonar, so far it looks like they haven't seen us, I don't see any aspect change in their profiles."

"Yes, they are ours, COB," Brian said. "But think about it for a minute. I tell Karen that we have a virus in our missile silos and can't raise command. She passes it on, I'm sure, to her boss, General Scott. Do you think he sits on it? No, I don't think so. Now we have two attack sardine cans headed our way. Coincidence?"

"Helm, Bridge," Brian said into his walkie. "Match the attack sub's aspect and speed, and do a slow, steady dive to the bottom. All good quiet. Let's go, COB, get below."

Brian and COB got down the ladders and closed both hatches as quietly as they could.

"Captain has the Conn," Haskins announced as Brian stepped back in the control room.

"I have the Conn," Brian said. "Reactor Room, Conn, reactor to quiet mode."

"Conn, Reactor Room, aye, sir, pumps off."

"Helm, take us down slow and steady until you match their depth," Brian said, "then cut the engines. And let us drift down to … Navigation, what's the bottom here?"

"Conn, Navigation, about 1,500 meters."

"Shallow, but it'll have to do," Brian said to himself out loud. "Helm, let it drift down to the bottom."

"Radio, Conn, you up yet?"

"Conn, Radio, aye, sir, all systems are up. We will have to either surface or float the buoy to reach command."

"Radio, Conn, acknowledged." Just then they settled on the bottom, soft and quiet. "Sonar, Conn, where are the attack subs?"

"Conn, Sonar, just above us, captain."

"Helm, get us off the bottom, nice and slow, and match their course and speed."

"Slow and steady, aye, sir."

"Conn, Sonar, they've both stopped directly above us."

"Helm, belay that last order. Let us sit."

"Aye, sir, engines off."

Who Owns Tomorrow?

"Sir, isn't there a chance that they're trying to find us to help?" COB asked.

"Not a chance in the world," Brian said. "If they wanted to help, they would have sent something out with better acoustics and less weaponry. These guys are here to do what they do."

Everyone concentrated on their station and tried to be as quiet as they could. Minutes ticked off. Five, then 10, then it was 15 minutes of silence.

"What the hell are they doing up there?" Haskins asked.

"Waiting for us to make a mistake," Brian said. "If they absolutely knew we were here, they would have started an attack run already. If they're just sitting there, they might have seen something on their sonar and are now trying to figure out if it's an echo or not."

"Conn, Sonar, they are both starting to move off, resuming their original course and speed."

"Okay, Helm, match their course and speed, just put us about halfway between them and the bottom, right where an echo would be. Reactor Room, Conn, leave the pumps off, but open the valves to let our movement bring in some water for the reactor."

"Conn, Reactor Room, aye, sir."

"With any luck, they will eventually increase speed and move off."

The big sub quietly lifted itself off the bottom, not even disturbing the mud and silt, and began to match the course and speed of the attack subs. Today's boomers were so quiet, even our own attack subs had trouble finding them sometimes.

"Helm, start to slow down gradually and descend. Slowly, as they move off. Let's let them get a few thousand yards past us before we try anything drastic. Report at 5,000 yards."

Brian's laptop was still on in his quarters and the USB drive was still plugged in. The virus began to re-infect the boat all over again.

Who Owns Tomorrow?

Chapter 9
Event minus 3 hours
DARPA Headquarters, Project Achilles

Karen looked at the clock on the wall of her office. It read 3:00. She and General Scott had been waiting for the IT crews to finish their virus scans so the fuel mixing could be restarted. The test was scheduled for 6:00 a.m. this morning, and if they missed the window, it might mean a long delay.

They had gotten everything started in her lab, picked up Sebastian from Dr. Sheffield's conference room bookshelf and come back to Karen's office.

She reached down and opened the bottom desk drawer on the right and took out a small mirror. It looked like a standard picture frame, maybe 8x10, but with a mirror set in the frame instead of a photo. She absently brushed the dust off the surface of the mirror and set it on the corner of her desk, away from her, closer to the general.

"What's that for?" the general asked, as he watched Karen fiddle with the mirror.

"You know," she said as she looked up at him, "I have no idea why I just did that. I've never used that mirror. Someone left it in this desk a long time ago."

General Scott shook his head, got up and poured himself another cup of coffee. He turned around and raised the pot up to Karen. She nodded and he walked over and filled her cup.

"This is getting old," she said.

"The coffee? I can make fresh." The general said.

"No, this …," she swept her arm around. "Just playing God without an instruction manual. There have been times when I wondered if I would make it home."

"I know," the general said. "I feel the same way sometimes. But what else can we do?"

"Simple," Karen said. "We can retire."

"You can't be serious. This is what you were born to do, I've never seen anyone better. You can't quit."

"Yes, I can," Karen said. "This is the perfect time. With this project done, and my reluctance to go on to get that first star, I'd say this is the best time."

"Well, we'd be losing one of our most innovative thinkers if that happens. Would you at least be interested in consulting, even from home?"

Before she could answer, the phone rang. It must have roused Sebastian from a deep sleep. He got up, stretched, and shook himself all over.

Karen picked up the phone as Sebastian meowed at her, trying to get her attention.

"This is Colonel Stiles," Karen said into the phone while pushing Sebastian away with the other hand.

She listened for a few moments and then hung up. "It was the guy in charge of the IT team scanning our servers." She said. "It's taking longer than they expected, and they're not even half way through yet. I don't like the sound of this at all."

Who Owns Tomorrow?

"I know," the general said. "I don't, either. Let me make a few calls, I'll be right back," and he left.

The other thing that had been bothering Karen was the persistent feeling of déjà vu. It had gotten worse over the last day or so, and it happened almost all the time, no matter what she was doing.

Sebastian jumped from the window sill to her lap and settled in for a good, long nap. She absently stroked the big tom as he purred and fell asleep. She thought about Brian in that damn submarine. In a couple of the rare arguments they had, she called it his big toy. Now she would be happy if he just got home alive. She knew he was good at what he did, but if they threw everything at you, all it took was one mistake.

He had even talked about retiring his commission after the next deployment. Perhaps they both could call it quits and quietly live the rest of their lives without any dangerous drama.

She was so deep in thought, she didn't hear General Scott come back into her office.

"Karen, … Karen," the general said.

"Oh, sorry," Karen said as she realized he was back. "I was lost in thought."

"Well, I have some good news," he said. "I've talked to our major supplier of the ingredients of the fuel you use, and they are ready to process another shipment of its major component as quickly as you need it. They can have it here in under 12 hours if your time needs to slip even a few hours."

"As long as the fuel we have is still viable, we'll be okay" Karen said. "If IT slides the time too far out doing the scan, it won't matter, we'll have to start mixing the fuel all over again."

"True," he said. "But that's the best I can do."

"I know," Karen said, "and I appreciate the effort, it might actually save the project."

"There is something else," the general said.

"What?" Karen asked. She stopped petting Sebastian.

"The two attack subs the Pentagon sent out after Brian's sub, … they can't find him," he said. "I think they're a little frustrated and aren't sure how to proceed."

Karen smiled. "I told you he was good," she said. "That's better news."

Who Owns Tomorrow?

"Karen." They both heard the voice from the corner of Karen's desk. It was the mirror. "Karen. Please look, this will be the last message."

It even startled Sebastian. He stood up on Karen's lap and looked at the mirror. General Scott got up and moved around to stand beside Karen so he could see the mirror.

There was something on the mirror. It looked like a subdued version of Karen holding up a large sign. Before they could tell what the message said, Sebastian jumped out of Karen's lap, slid across the desk and knocked the mirror off to the floor. Karen and General Scott looked at each other in horror as the big tom bounded out of Karen's office and down the hall.

Karen ran over to pick up the pieces of the mirror while General Scott called Dr. Sheffield.

"Dr. Sheffield," the general said, "we've had another message in Karen's office."

"On my way," Sheffield said.

Karen had all the pieces of the mirror on her desk by the time Dr. Sheffield got to her office.

"Was it like the first one?" he asked. "A message on a mirror?"

"Yes," Karen said, pointing to the pile of broken glass. "That's what's left of it."

"Did you get a chance to see the message?" Sheffield asked.

"No," General Scott said. "We were just getting to it when it got knocked off the desk."

"Let me guess," Sheffield said, looking around. "That damn cat."

"I know you don't like cats, Dr. Sheffield, but focus. Can you detect what the message was on the remains of this mirror?"

Dr. Sheffield huffed his distaste at the little animal.

"Alright, alright … it is possible to detect the tachyon pattern if they are still using the same technology and if we have enough of the surface the beam hit." Sheffield scooped up all the pieces and headed toward the door.

"I don't need to tell you, doctor," General Scott said as Sheffield was on his way out the door, "this has priority over everything."

"I'll let you know what I find," Sheffield said over his shoulder.

"Well," the general said, "what do we do now? Do you want to dump the virus scans and restart your project?"

"No, not yet," Karen said. "I need to know what that message was before we do anything. We've been shooting in the dark since this thing started, and I hope this is a complete, readable message."

Who Owns Tomorrow?

Chapter 10
Event plus 16 hours
Remains of DARPA Headquarters

"Are we ready for the next transmission?" Karen asked, coming back into Sheffield's conference room. She had been in the adjoining office trying to get some sleep. Sheffield had turned his actual office into a dorm room of sorts while they were trying to figure out what to do. Karen didn't think he had slept since this started.

She had slept little, and when she did sleep it was filled with nightmares of what was to come and thoughts of losing Brian. She was sure he was gone. She didn't think anyone or anything had survived, save what was within the shield they hid behind.

She looked around and saw Sebastian sitting on his stack of books on the one remaining bookcase. He had never really been a cuddly cat and had always been a little standoffish. She still wondered why he had been so insistent on coming with her.

"Yes, I think so," he said. "Are you sure that the mirror is going to be on her desk?"

"I'm the one who put it there, I should hope so," Karen said with a slight laugh. "At the time, I had no idea why I wanted it there, but now it's obvious. Is the future influencing the past somehow? Nudging it along a certain path? Or is what happened in the past influencing us to do the same thing we experienced in that timeline?"

"We're all stumbling around in the dark where this is concerned," Sheffield said. "All we really know is we can transmit a signal into the past that, for now, is only evident on a mirror. It would be interesting to explore whether a person could influence him, or herself in the past, but I wouldn't even know where to start, and I'm positive we don't have the time right now."

"It would be a lot simpler if we could just *think* to ourselves in the past what it is we want them to do," Karen said.

"I thought you were generally opposed to us trying to change the past?" Sheffield asked.

"I still think it's a mistake, that we're playing God trying to mess with the timeline, especially with our own past, but it would at least be simpler than what we're doing now."

"Go ahead and sit in the same spot," Dr. Sheffield said. "We want to try to be as consistent as possible."

Karen sat down where she sat for the first transmission, grabbed the legal pad on the corner of the table and started writing.

"What are you doing?" Sheffield asked.

"We're going to try something a little more direct this time," Karen said. "They know who I am and they've been through this once already. I don't need to waste time pussyfooting around like we did with the last message."

Who Owns Tomorrow?

Sheffield looked at what she had written on the legal pad.

It was pretty simple. Only two lines in large print. It said *Don't delay Project Achilles, no matter what happens. The shield must come up on time, at 6:00 a.m.*

"The reason the full message didn't get through last time was we started by saying too much and ran out of time," Karen said. "That's not going to happen this time."

"You know we didn't run out of time," Dr. Sheffield said. "It was that damn cat of yours. He did the same thing to us trying to receive this message in our timeline."

"Maybe this time, it'll go differently. All we can do is try."

"You really think this will help?" Dr. Sheffield said.

"From what I see, it can't hurt," Karen said.

"Okay, here we go," Dr. Sheffield said. The tachyon emitter was a relatively small device that sat on the other end of the conference table, pointed to nowhere in particular. Or, so it seemed. Dr. Sheffield had spent quite a lot of time calculating exactly where the earth would have been at the precise moment Karen would be sitting in her office a few hours before the test, and the exact coordinates of her office desk. The orientation of the earth with respect to where they were now didn't matter. The particles would go through everything and bathe her entire desk. Or, rather, they would bathe the spot in space where her desk was in the past. The fact that the particles traveled faster than the speed of light did the rest. Since the mirror was the only reflective surface on the desk, that's where the vision would appear. "We will only have about 15 seconds this time. If we do any more than that the generators will not be able to handle the tachyon emitter and the shield at the same time."

"Okay," Karen said. "All I'm going to do is hold up the sign, call out her name, and tell her to look at the sign. We have to get her attention right away so she'll look at the mirror. If she left the cat at home this time, she will have just enough time to restart the fuel mixing process, and start the shield reactors before the world falls apart."

"Everyone stand by," Dr. Sheffield said. He started the camera and the tachyon emitter at the same time.

Who Owns Tomorrow?

The transmission lasted only about 15 seconds, just enough time to get their message across. Any more time would have compromised the generators that were keeping the shield up.

When the transmission was over, Karen and Dr. Sheffield just sat for a few minutes, waiting.

"Would something have happened already?" Karen asked.

"Probably," Dr. Sheffield said. "My guess is if it worked at all, no matter how long it took them to figure it out, we would not be sitting here discussing it like this. We'd be gone almost instantly after sending the message out."

"So you think that means Sebastian did the same thing in their timeline as he did in ours?"

"I think that's the only explanation. He knocked the mirror off again, and it took them too long to figure out what the message was."

"Is fate against us?" Karen asked.

"What are you talking about?" Dr. Sheffield asked.

"It seems like everything we try fails for one reason or another. Maybe the past just can't be changed. No matter what we do, the past will work out as it happened, no matter what."

"You'd better hope that's not the way things work," Dr. Sheffield said.

Karen heard one of the generators falter and shut down. She knew exactly what the sound was. She had heard it enough every time they tested the generators. Although now, it meant a lot more than in those tests that seemed so long ago. The shield walls moved in a little in response to the decrease of available power.

"It looks like it's getting close," Dr. Sheffield said. "Didn't all the generators have about the same amount of fuel?"

"Yes, pretty much," Karen said. "Some may have had a little more than others, but not much."

Karen looked at the darkness beyond the shield. Neither of them knew if it was really dark out there or if that was just another function of the shield itself. She remembered when the shield first went up, she could see through it with no problem. And before, when the debris hit the shield, it was all visible. Perhaps things were changing over time. Perhaps everything really was gone. After all, this was the first test. They had no idea what was really left out there.

They didn't even know if they were already in the rift or outside it, drifting in the nothingness.

Another generator stopped and the south shield wall moved into the conference room just a few feet from where they were. She had thought about this often. How would the end come when it happened? Would the shield just dissolve away when the first generator failed or would it cease to exist a piece at a time? Getting smaller and smaller. And not really knowing what lay beyond the shield, all they could do was speculate about what would happen when all the generators failed.

"I think we should move into the server room where the shield control is," Karen said. "That may give us a little more time."

Karen grabbed Sebastian off his favorite stack of books. As they got up and moved across the north hallway into the server room, another generator stopped and the shield was now only covering the server room where the shield controller itself was and the room immediately to the north of the server room that housed the generators and fuel tanks.

Dr. Sheffield settled onto a couch along the back wall and Karen dropped Sebastian on the chair opposite. Dr. Sheffield hadn't said anything since the generator failures started. Karen went into the backup server room where the generators were and checked on the fuel tank for the remaining two generators. Surprised to find it a quarter full, she went back in the shield control room and checked the shield's control panel.

"Based on how much fuel the remaining generators are using and how much fuel we have left, I think we have about two hours left before they run out of fuel," Karen said, plopping down next to Sebastian.

"Might as well just turn if off at this point," Sheffield said. "We don't have the power or the time to contact the past again, so there's nothing else we can do."

"Do we just cease to exist or do we continue as our selves in the past?" Karen asked. "They now know about us, they know we've been trying to contact them. What do they think about us just going away, ceasing to exist?"

"They have no idea what will happen to us, if they're even thinking about that at all," Sheffield said. "Remember what you were doing 24 hours ago and how you felt about your future self when she contacted you? The same thing that happened to you is happening to them. And will happen to their past selves. And so on, until someone figures out a way to stop this madness by stopping the disaster."

Sebastian had settled into the crook of Karen's arm and had fallen asleep. That cat could sleep anywhere.

She didn't really believe, contrary to what Dr. Sheffield thought, that Sebastian was preventing them from contacting the past in time to stop the disaster. How could a cat possibly know that you shouldn't mess with the past and even try to stop you from doing so?

She still wasn't sure what she believed about the past. Could you really change it or not? And would this really keep going on time after time until someone did change the past? She just wasn't sure about any of it. At least not as sure as Dr. Sheffield seemed to be. All she was sure about was that Sebastian wasn't intentionally stopping them from changing the past. He was just a cat, how could he do that?

She looked over at Sheffield on the couch. He was mumbling to himself, madly scribbling away on a legal pad. What was he thinking? There was no way for them to contact the past again. It was up to the people in her past to try and fix this now.

Just as Sebastian started purring, the remainder of the generators stopped, a lot earlier than she thought they should. Or perhaps she had been lost in thought longer than she knew. They watched as the shield got dimmer and dimmer and then evaporated altogether.

Almost immediately, it was as if a tornado had formed in the room. Papers, furniture, parts of the walls, actually anything not nailed down began to swirl around them and eventually began pushing them toward the Project Darkness lab across the south hall. In reality, everything was headed for where the Project Darkness lab used to be. Hell, the hallway wasn't even there any more.

The rift was now huge. It was so large, you couldn't even see the top or bottom, and it looked wider than anything she had ever seen before. It was a tear in the fabric of space itself, and it was bright white inside now. You couldn't see anything inside. It was so big, there were only two things still left as far as she could see. The pitiful little piece of real estate they occupied and the rift itself.

Sebastian was holding on to her for dear life and the last thing Karen thought before she and Sebastian sailed into the rift was, *I wonder if Brian's on the other side?*

Who Owns Tomorrow?

Chapter 11

"Okay, everyone," Brian said, "we need to make some decisions, and we need to make them rather quickly." He was at the head of the table in the officers' mess. Around him were COB, Lt. Haskins, Lt. Garrison, and Petty Officer Lee. It had only been about five minutes since they had successfully evaded the two Los Angeles class attack subs, and they were at zero bubble about 1,000 feet off the bottom waiting for the attack subs to get at least 5,000 yards out in front of them before they moved again. Lt. Randall, the communications officer, had the Conn.

Brian picked up the mic off the wall hook and said, "Sonar, Captain, where are the attack subs?"

"Captain, Sonar, they are about 3,000 yards out and still moving slowly away from us."

"Sonar, Captain, keep me posted."

"Captain, Sonar, aye, sir."

"Reactor Room, Captain," Brian said.

"Captain, Reactor Room."

"Turn half the pumps back on for the reactor," Brian said. "We'll do them all when the attack subs get farther out."

"Aye, sir."

"Lee, assuming the virus is still able to re-infect the boat, how much time do you think we have?"

[118]

"Sir, since we don't really know when or from where the virus was introduced, we don't know how long it took to get as far as it did the first time. But, if I had to guess, I'd stay conservative and say probably only about 30 to 45 minutes to get to where we were at the worst."

"That's not much time," Brian said. He picked up the mic again.

"Conn, Captain, are communications still up?"

Lt. Randall looked over at the radio operator and he gave Randall the thumbs up.

"Captain, Conn, we're still up." Randall replied.

Brain put the mic back on the wall. "We're damn sure not surfacing just yet and floating the buoy would make too much noise. Any suggestions?"

"We can wait a bit longer and try going to periscope depth," COB said. "The VHF antenna will break the surface at that depth."

"I had considered that," Brian said, "and I still might go there. It all depends on how we feel about our friends out there. I still don't think they're out here to try to communicate with us."

"At the very least," COB said, "we can talk to Command and let them know we have control of the boat and they might call off the dogs."

"Well, we have control for now," Lee said. "I don't think that's going to last that long."

"What if we did a hard reset like the last time every 20 minutes or so?" Lt. Garrison, the XO, asked.

Who Owns Tomorrow?

"We could keep doing that while we're looking for whatever device might still be on that's propagating the virus."

"I would consider that," Brian said, "but only as long as we can call off the dogs first. We need to be on the surface to do a reset, you know that, and we can't risk it unless we can get with Command and have them call off the attack subs first. What can we do to figure out where the virus is coming from?"

"About the only thing you can do," Lee said, "is to just go compartment by compartment looking for any device that's on and connected to the network that might still be giving the virus a path to the boat."

"I'll put out a boat-wide message to the crew to turn off any and all electronics and you put together a team of men to go compartment by compartment to make sure we get them all. If we can find the source of the virus, that'll go a long way to making sure we come out of this in one piece."

"Aye, Captain," Lee said, and headed out.

Brian grabbed the mic off the wall next to his seat and switched it to 1MC. "All hands, this is the Captain," he said. "Our beloved boat, the Ridge Runner, is once again put in harm's way. We are currently being dogged by two of our own Los Angeles class attack boats. I'm sure you are all aware by now that we have a virus on board whose intent appears to be to launch a missile. We cannot effectively deal with the virus until we get the attack subs off our back, and we can't really do that until we get communications capability. There is a team of men coming around to all compartments to make sure we don't have any non-*Tennessee* related electronics turned on that might be contributing to the virus problem. Please make sure all non-standard electronics are turned off and cooperate fully with the team led by Petty Officer Lee."

"Sonar, Captain, where are our friends?"

"Captain, Sonar, they are just under 5,000 yards out and still on the same course and speed. They don't appear to have spotted us at all."

"Conn, Captain, Mr. Randall, start us up again, nice and slow, and get us to periscope depth. Continue to match the attack sub's course."

"Captain, Conn, aye, sir."

"Radio, Captain, as soon as we are at periscope depth, raise the antennas and see if you can get Atlantic Command."

"Captain, Radio, aye, sir."

"Okay," Brian said as he turned back to the officers in the room. "I think what we will try to do is contact Atlantic Command and let them know we have control of the boat. Hopefully, that will convince them to call off the dogs, and we can continue to do a reset every 20 minutes or so until we find the source of the virus. If I can I would like to avoid a shooting war with two attack boats. Any other questions?"

No one said anything.

Who Owns Tomorrow?

"Here's hoping this works," Brian said. "Let's get back up to the control room."

On his way back up to the control room, Brian thought of the old ditty the crew members of the fast attack boats used to say.

Fast attack tough,
Ain't no slack in fast attack,
Ain't no pride in a Trident ride,
Boomers - on patrol going two knots to nowhere.

If it came to it, they might just show them how things had changed in the last 20 years. The attack boats were essentially the way they were 20 years ago, but there had been many changes to the ballistic subs over those years that were under wraps. In a lot of respects there might not be any contest any more between the two.

"Captain has the Conn," Lt. Randall said as Brian walked back into the control room."

"Captain has the Conn," Brian repeated.

COB was standing behind the helmsman in his usual position, Lt. Haskins, the weapons officer, was at the missile console next to Petty Officer Lee's position, and Lt. Garrison, the XO, was standing next to Brian beside the twin periscopes.

"Where are we, COB?" Brian asked.

"We are about 175 feet below the surface," COB said.

Brian picked up the mic, "Sonar, Conn, where are our friends?"

"Conn, Sonar, still on the same course, same speed, about 7,000 yards out."

"Almost four miles," Brian thought out loud. "Radio, Conn, extend the antenna."

"Conn, Radio, aye, sir."

They listened to the quiet *whirr* sound as the antenna slowly broke the surface of the water.

"Sonar, Conn, any aspect change on the attack dogs?"

"Conn, Sonar, they're slowing down, sir."

"Crap," Brian said. "All stop, all good quiet."

"Conn, Sonar, they are surfacing, Captain."

"That means they saw something they didn't understand on sonar," Brian said. "Everyone, just sit tight and let's see if they dive again and get back to their original course and speed."

Everyone was quiet.

"Radio, Conn, stay on their frequency, see what you can pick up," Brian said.

"Conn, Radio, aye, sir." The radio operator sat quietly, just listening. "They're contacting Atlantic Command asking for confirmation of orders. They think they've seen evidence of us a few miles out on sonar, but they can't be sure. Silence. Nothing, there's still a long pause, Sir. Here they come. Command says that before they do anything, they have to absolutely verify the target. They must be sure it's us. They just broke off, sir, that's it."

"Conn, Sonar, they are reversing course and heading our way, but still very slowly."

"They want to see what their ghost does," Brian said. "Helm, sit tight for a few minutes." Brian picked up the mic. "Forward Torpedo Room, Conn, load the BSADS."

"Conn, Forward Torpedo Room, aye, sir."

The BSADS (Ballistic Submarine Acoustic Defense System) was a projectile under its own power and control whose job was to evade hunter-killer attack subs by constantly running away from their sonar and presenting the profile of a full-sized ballistic submarine.

Most submariners just called it a *stand-in*. It was developed in the mid-2020s in response to Russian work on the same idea. Everyone in the submarine business knew of its existence and its capabilities, but how well it worked depended on how experienced the captain chasing it was.

The idea was really simple. In a real fight, you would deploy the stand-in and sit still and quiet until it was fully deployed and began moving. As soon as it moved, you would move in the opposite direction and the enemy wouldn't know which was which. It would improve your odds simply by the fact that now there were two of you and that was enough to muddy the waters, so to speak.

"Radio, Conn, can we get a message out?" Brian asked.

"Conn, Radio, wait one."

"Forward Torpedo Room, Conn, stand by," Brian said.

"Conn, Radio, sir, we're back to the static on the outbound channels. We can receive everything, it seems, but can't send anything out."

Damn, Brian thought, we took too long. Or the virus learned from its last trip. "Lee, Conn, how's progress?" He asked into the mic.

"Conn, Lee, slow, sir. We're just now heading to the officer's quarters."

Who Owns Tomorrow?

"Is it possible for the virus to actually do damage that would still be around after the reset?" Brian asked.

"Possible, but unlikely in our situation," Lee replied. "If you're seeing evidence of its presence like we saw before, chances are it's just back already and is reintegrating itself into the boat."

Brian thought quickly. That meant they would need to do another reset to get rid of it again. But that would really do no good, long term, unless Lee and his team could find where the virus was coming from. But they couldn't do the reset until they could safely get to the surface.

"Forward Torpedo Room, Conn, launch the stand-in. Radio, Conn, retract the antenna."

"Aye, sir," from both the torpedo room and the radio operator.

The control room was quiet as they listened to the antenna retract and the stand-in launch. Brian was hoping the attack subs couldn't tell the difference between the two sounds and they would be confused enough to give the stand-in time to fully deploy.

"Conn, Sonar, targets are increasing speed toward us. They just crossed the 5,000 yard mark."

The stand-in began deployment almost completely silently after it was launched. It unfolded itself forward, away from its propulsion unit to almost the full size of a ballistic submarine. The material on its reinforced frame was designed to reflect as much sonar as possible to make it look as though it was larger than it really was. In the open waters of the Atlantic, the stand-in could operate for a full 24 hours before it started to either deteriorate or run out of fuel, depending on how much it moved. As soon as it was completely deployed, its control system determined where the active sonar was coming from and it immediately headed in the opposite direction, just like a real target would.

"Lt. Haskins, release the sonar shield," Brian said as the stand-in began to move and put distance between them. The sonar shield was a completely new toy to cut the odds ever further in their favor.

"Aye, sir," Haskins said.

Lt. Haskins entered the commands on his console to open tiny shield deployment ports on the surface of the *Tennessee*. This was a modification to the *Tennessee's* skin that happened on their last in-port retrofit. No one knew about it outside of the captain and his weapons officer, Lt. Haskins, and it was to be tested on this run along with the new missile propellant. Nothing like a field test under fire.

The shield retrofit added a new skin onto the *Tennessee* over the existing one. It extended over most of the top, both sides, and the bottom of the sub and covered about 80% of its surface area. The only parts that weren't covered were the screws aft, the sonar array forward, and all the area around all the torpedo and missile hatches. The new skin was a few millimeters thick and was filled with a new, proprietary graphene compound. When the deployment ports opened, the semi-liquid, semi-metal compound oozed out and expanded to cover almost the entire boat. The water pressure kept it stuck to the boat and its major property was that it absorbed almost all sound waves. This was supposed to be a test, but used in combination with the BSADS masquerade device, it just might give them the edge they needed.

"Sonar, Conn, just passive sonar from here on out," Brian said into the mic.

"Conn, Sonar, aye, sir. The targets are slowing. Moving at to a crawl. Now they've stopped."

"They can't figure out what just happened," Brian said. "Their sonar screens were going crazy while the BSADS was being deployed and our sonar shield went up. Now things have settled down and the BSADS is starting to move away from them. They're just making sure they're following the right target."

The two Los Angeles class attack subs were close to 4,000 yards out and now began to make two separate attack runs.

"Conn, Sonar, they're diverging, sir, one is following the stand-in, directly behind it, and closing the gap now at 3,500 yards, and the other seems to be circling around to the north."

"Sonar, Conn, default attack pattern," Brian said. "Does it even look like they see us?"

"Conn, Sonar, no, sir, they're just ignoring us."

The *Tennessee* suddenly lurched forward and rolled left as the engines went into full and the rudder brought them about sharply.

"Helm, what the hell is this?" Brian asked in their general direction.

"Not us, sir," COB said. The helm operators were frantically trying to get control of the boat. It had leveled off but was still headed north at a good clip.

"Sonar, Conn, where are our friends?" Brian asked.

"Conn, Sonar, one of them is still after the stand-in and we're headed straight for the one that was circling around."

"Sonar, Conn, how far?"

"Conn, Sonar, about 2,000 yards and closing."

Brian was frantically trying to figure out what the virus was up to. Then it hit him. It had to eliminate the attack subs before it could even try to launch a missile. It was going after the first attack sub, the farthest one out. They would never know what hit them in the mode they were in now. The new shield made them almost invisible.

The virus didn't know the attack subs couldn't see them. All Brian was trying to do was evade them. The virus was going to destroy them.

"Is there any way we can get rid of this shield?" Brian yelled over to Lt. Haskins.

Who Owns Tomorrow?

"Not as far as I know, sir," Haskins said. "It is a prototype and has no controls to speak of. It's only good for one application, but we'll have to ride it out."

"Sonar, Conn, how far?

"Conn, Sonar, just a little over 1,500 yards."

"Sir, the auto-loader has just loaded a torpedo into forward tube 1," Lt. Haskins yelled.

"What the hell is going on?" Brian asked to no one in particular.

Petty Officer Lee had just come into the control room, holding up Brian's flash drive.

"Where did you get that?" Brian asked.

Lee walked up close to Brian and said quietly, "It was still in your laptop in your quarters, sir," he said. "That's where the virus was coming from. The way these things work, it most likely jumped onto your flash drive at the base before we left."

"Damnit," Brian said, "so it was me all along?"

"No," COB said, "it was the virus all along, it just hitchhiked onto the boat on your drive." He had been close enough to hear everything.

"At any rate," Brian said, "I should have known better."

"Let's just fix it," COB said. "That's the first order of business."

"Sir, the torpedo has armed itself in the tube, it's getting ready to fire," Haskins said.

"Sonar, Conn, go active. Give me a couple of pings," Brian said.

"Conn, Sonar, aye, sir." Two pings sprang out of nowhere as far as the attack subs were concerned.

"Conn, Sonar, the sub that was following the stand-in has stopped. My guess is they're trying to figure out what the hell is going on. The one that was circling around to the north is still on the move. Wait, the one that was chasing the stand-in directly has fired a torpedo at it, probably to eliminate that threat so he can figure out what else is going on."

The torpedo hit the stand-in and exploded, destroying it instantly. But there was no buckling bulkhead noise, no ripping sounds, and no water rushing in. This probably told the captain of the attack sub it had been a dummy.

"Conn, Sonar, now he's turned in our direction trying to figure out where the pings came from. He's just sitting."

"Torpedo away," Lt. Haskins said. "It was already armed and now has acquired the sub closest to us, the one that had circled around to the north. The attack sub sees it and has started to try to maneuver away. I don't think it's going to make it. Impact in 45 seconds."

"We didn't warn it fast enough," Brian said. "Sonar, Conn, what's the other sub doing?"

"Conn, Sonar, it's still just sitting where it had destroyed the stand-in. I think it's even more confused. It's using active sonar trying to find us, but it can't yet. We aren't where the pings came from anymore and the torpedo launch confuses things even more. Now the torpedo is off the screen, so they don't know what the hell is going on."

"Torpedo impact in 35 seconds," Lt. Haskins said.

The torpedo itself used passive sonar to home in on its target initially. It was a gas turbine model with sound silencing modifications, so chances were the attack sub wouldn't even know it was about to be hit until it was too late. The torpedo would wait until it was too close for the target to do anything about it and then turn on its active sonar to make sure it detonated at just the right spot, several meters right below the sub.

"Torpedo impact in 20 seconds," Lt. Haskins said.

"Lt. Garrison, head to the forward torpedo room and Lt. Randall, the aft," Brian said. "Manually lock out all the outer doors, if the virus tries to fire another torpedo, it'll probably take us out instead. That's all I can think of right now." Brian took off his cap and threw it on the floor. "Dammit, I can't believe we're about to sink one of our own boats."

"Torpedo impact in 15 seconds," Lt. Haskins said.

"Sir, it's not us," COB said. "You're doing everything you can to stop this virus, it's just too sadistic."

"Ten seconds," Haskins said.

Just about now, the torpedo was switching to active sonar and the attack sub would know it was there. There was no way to outrun or out-maneuver it. It was as though the torpedo just wanted everyone on the target boat to know their time was up.

It zeroed in on its target and tilted its nose down a couple of degrees to get underneath the boat. It detonated just about five meters under the boat, and the shock wave cracked the primary and secondary hulls almost immediately. The rips in the hulls allowed the shock wave and tons of seawater to rush into the boat, killing almost the entire crew right away. A few seconds after the initial shockwave, the air bubble created by the blast collapsed and a huge jet of water ripped through the boat at supersonic speed, actually breaking the boat in half.

Both halves started to slowly sink and then settled on the bottom. Any of the crew who were not killed by the shock of the blast would eventually run out of air. There was no way to get to them.

"Conn, Sonar, hull's breaking up and buckling. Boat is in pieces on the bottom."

The control room got very quiet. Normally when this happened there would be cheers of joy as we sank an

Who Owns Tomorrow?

enemy boat and were safe. That we did the job our country asked us to do, to protect it. That wasn't the case this time. The crew had just destroyed one of their own boats and killed their own comrades in arms. The fact that the *Tennessee* had been compromised and taken over by an enemy virus didn't lighten the mood one bit.

"Sonar, Conn, where's the second sub?" Brian asked as he picked up his hat off the floor.

"Conn, Sonar, it's still sitting right where it was. I think they're still confused about where the torpedo came from, I don't think they know where we are."

"Captain, what about the stingers?" COB asked.

"They don't really have ports that can be closed, I don't think the virus could affect them," Brian said. "They're in their own ports in various places around the boat and there is no manual override for them."

Stingers were small projectiles of depleted uranium strategically placed around the hull of the boat, each with its own miniature propulsion system. Some of them were armed, some weren't. They were intended to be used in close quarters, where a torpedo wasn't a viable option. They would punch right through the sonar shield without any problem and could disable an enemy's propulsion system by breaking propellers, or shut down his sonar by cracking or breaking the sonar node at the front of the boat.

"Yes, I know," COB said. "I meant, can we use them against the other attack sub to just disable it instead of the virus trying to destroy it?"

"Haskins, are we completely compromised as far as weapons systems again?" Brian asked.

[135]

Who Owns Tomorrow?

"Yes, sir, we are pretty much like last time," Haskins said. "None of the remaining torpedoes have been loaded, so somehow the virus knows we've manually locked the outer doors."

"Lee, is that possible?" Brian asked.

"Sir, the only thing I can think of is the circuit that reports that the outer door is locked," Les said. "The virus must be monitoring that somehow."

"How about the stingers?" Brian asked. "Can we fire those?"

"We can," Haskins said. "They are mostly mechanical, but we'd have to be able to maneuver to the right spot."

"How about the missile silos?" Brian asked. "Are they still quiet?"

"None of them have begun to spin up yet," Haskins said. "That will be our first indication, and if this is like the last time, it'll be silo 14."

Brian turned around and faced the Helm.

"How about maneuvering?" he asked COB. "We still down?"

"Aye, sir, we are," COB said. "The only thing we have that will move us are the chicken switches."

"I don't want to surface just yet," Brian said. "Even though we don't want to kill the attack sub, they have orders to kill us. If we start to move too much, they will see us, even with the sonar shield."

"Why isn't the virus spinning up the missile and moving to launch depth?" Haskins asked.

"Probably for the same reason," Brian said. "I think somehow it knows if it does that now, the attack sub will destroy us before it can launch."

"So, it's having the same problem we are," Haskins said. "but for different reasons."

"Radio, Conn," Brian said into the mic.

"Conn, Radio, aye, sir."

"Radio, Conn, can we make some external noise with the cable that floats the buoy and by raising and lowering the antennas? Those are completely manual systems, right?"

Silence for a few seconds.

"Conn, Radio, yes sir, we can, but that would give away our position."

"Radio, Conn, that's what I'm counting on," Brian said. "Stand by with buoy winch and main antenna."

"What do you have in mind?" COB asked.

"I'm going to see if I can make the attack sub come to us," Brian said. "If we're careful, he will position himself so we can damage his propulsion system, and he won't be able to maneuver to get a shot at us."

"You're hoping that if we disable him, the virus will leave him alone?" COB asked.

"That's the thought," Brian said. "That and the fact that we can't possibly try to surface even using the chicken switches unless we know that attack sub is either not there or disabled. His first priority is to take us out and as soon as we surface, the new liquid shield we are trying goes away."

"So the plan is the same as last time?" COB asked. "Try to surface quickly and do a reset once we're there?"

"Yes," Brian said. "Unless anyone else has any other ideas?"

"Sir," Haskins yelled from the weapons station, "whatever we do, we need to do fast. Silo 14 is coming online in pre spin-up mode."

"How much time do we have?" Brian asked.

"My guess is about four minutes," Haskins said.

"Sonar, Conn, where's our friend?" Brian asked into the mic.

"Conn, Sonar, he's about the same place he was before, off our port side, about 1,500 yards away. Just sitting."

"Sonar, Conn, keep sounding out the numbers. Radio, start raising the low-gain antenna. Slowly."

The crew in the control room could hear the low-gain antenna begin to move. It made noise. It would be hard to miss on passive sonar. That was what Brian was banking on.

"Helm, any change in our position?" Brian asked the helmsman.

"No change," COB said.

"Conn, Sonar, he's turning in our direction, but no movement toward us yet."

"Radio, Conn, let the winch out slowly," Brian said.

More noise, still relatively quiet, but definitely discernible to a sophisticated sonar rig.

"Conn, Sonar, he's moving in our direction. It's hesitant, with starts and stops, but he's slowly coming this way."

"Radio, Conn, stop all noise."

After a few seconds, "Conn, Sonar, he's stopped. Obviously all he sees on his sonar is the noise we're making, he sees no larger profile. When the noise stops, so does he."

"Radio, Conn, he's started again, slowly. I still don't think he sees us, he's just trying to figure out what the noise is. It's not going to match anything in his profiles."

"Sonar, Conn, let me know when he's right on top of us."

Everyone was quiet, just waiting for word from sonar.

"Helm, we still in the same place?" Brian asked.

"We've drifted a little aft, but essentially in the same place," COB said. "Why isn't the virus doing anything?"

"Lee?" Brian asked.

Who Owns Tomorrow?

"Not sure, sir, this is all new territory. This is a very sophisticated set of code. My only speculation is that, somehow, the virus has determined that the target attack sub cannot see us. It might have to do with the fact that since it hasn't attacked yet, it's extrapolating that it cannot see us."

"Haskins, silo 14 in spin-up yet?" Brian asked

"About three minutes," Haskins said.

"How long do we have after it starts spin-up?"

"About another two minutes, maybe less," Haskins said. "That's never a set time, it depends on the missile. It could be plus or minus as much as seven or eight seconds."

"Conn, Sonar, the target is just about on top of us now. He's slowing to a complete stop. My guess is that he knows he's at the source of the sound, but still can't figure out what it is."

"Sonar, Conn, where are the screws?" Brian asked.

"Conn, Sonar, they are aft of us about 35 yards."

"Forward Torpedo Room, Conn, open and close the inside door of one of the torpedo tubes a couple of times. Make a good amount of noise, then stop."

"Conn, Forward Torpedo Room, aye, sir."

"Haskins, Lee, get ready on the stinger controls. When Sonar says the screws are actually above us, pop all the stingers on top of us."

"Sonar, Conn, count off the yards."

"Conn, Sonar, aye, sir."

[140]

The crew in the forward torpedo room opened and slammed the door on one of the torpedo tubes a couple of times. You could hear it all over the sub, not just in the control room.

"Conn, Sonar, he's moving forward. 30 yards. Now 20, now 15, now seven. Now, sir, he's right on top of us."

Haskins and Lee fired all the stingers on top of the Tennessee. About half of them were just depleted uranium. Those fired first, and the other half were tipped with small explosive charges. The theory was what the hardened stingers didn't break, the explosives would. They could hear them hit various parts of the attack sub, and it sounded like the explosive-tipped projectiles hit the screws dead center. You could actually hear the scraping metal sound as the screws were bent forward and began hitting the body of the sub. Then they stopped altogether.

"Conn, Sonar, it worked, sir, they had to shut down the screws and will probably be surfacing shortly. They will have to stay on battery until they get help."

It was clear that everyone in the control room was feeling better about how things were working out. There were collective sighs of relief and hand shakes and fist-bumps all over the room.

"Settle down, everyone," Brian said. "Obviously we accomplished what we needed to do to disable the attack sub without destroying it. And hopefully making it a non-threat to the virus. Now, let's do the rest of this plan. Everyone, hold on. Haskins, what's the status of silo 14?"

"It's in spin-up, sir, it's going to be close."

"Haskins," Brian said, "get down to silo 14 and disconnect it, even if you have to do it the same way you did before. Lee, get ready to shut down the rest of the weapons systems, we'll handle communications and the helm."

"Aye, sir, on my way," Haskins said as he left the control room.

"Helm, emergency blow!!" Brian said.

The helmsman stood up and grabbed both chicken switches and pulled them both up, manually blowing compressed air from the storage tanks into the main ballast tanks. Immediately, just like the last time, the boat lost several million pounds of water ballast and the front of the boat tilted up and began to surface quickly.

"Any reaction?" Brian asked.

"No," COB said. He sounded confused. "There is no response this time, we're headed for the surface and will be there in just a few seconds."

As the boat broke through the surface and settled its nose on the choppy water, the crew started to shut down all the major components of the boat.

But this time, nothing was working. As they shut down a component and restarted it, it was obvious that the virus was still there.

"Lee, what the hell's going on?" Brian asked

"I have no idea, sir. Obviously, the virus has found a way to stay in control of the major components even though they have been restarted. It is adapting."

"Haskins," Brian said into the mic, "did you get silo 14 shut down?"

"Yes," Haskins replied. "I had to do the same thing I did before, but it's offline."

Who Owns Tomorrow?

Just then, the boat shuddered and it dropped a couple of inches at the middle as silo 13 launched its missile. The compressed steam load popped the ballistic missile out of its tube and up about 25 feet above the surface of the boat. As it started to drop back toward the open hatch of its tube, the first stage solid-fuel rocket engine fired and it began to gain altitude. The tube hatch and two hatches on either side of that missile tube were melted and essentially fused onto the surface of the boat as the engine fired so close to the boat on the surface.

"Haskins," Brian yelled into the mic. "What the hell was that?"

"Sir," Lee said from his weapons station, "I believe the virus sent signals showing it was silo 14 that was spinning up when in fact it was silo 13. We just launched one of the duds."

"Haskins," Brian tried again. "Haskins, come in. Lee, get down there and see what's going on."

"Aye, sir," Lee said on his way out of the control room.

"Helm, any response to the shutdown?" Brian asked.

"No, sir," COB said. "We're still not in control."

"Radio, Conn, does anything work on your end?"

"No, sir, neither outbound or inbound."

"Sonar, Conn, report all contacts. Are you still up?" Brian asked

"Conn, Sonar, yes, sir, I'm still up and all I can see is the attack sub. It hasn't surfaced yet and is still sitting on the bottom. It looks to be disabled. It's not moving."

"Surface Radar, Conn, can you track that missile?"

"Yes, sir, we're still up. It looks like its telemetry is off, it's not gaining altitude like it should."

"Can you tell where it's headed?" Brian asked.

"All I can tell, sir, is it's headed for the D.C. area. I can't get any more specific than that."

Haskins and Lee walked into the control room just as Brian was finishing with Radar. Haskins looked a little shaken.

"What happened?" Brian asked.

"I wasn't ready for it, and the launch tossed me into one of the bulkheads. I'm okay now. Lee was telling me that the virus was sending us phony info about which missile was going to launch."

"Yeah, that's what it looked like. At least it was a dud and it's headed for the D.C. area somewhere. Shouldn't be too much damage."

Just then, the boat started a descent, slow but deliberate.

"Helm, what's our status?" Brian asked.

"Ten degree down bubble, engines are at one third," COB replied. "If I didn't know any better, I'd say we were headed for the bottom."

Who Owns Tomorrow?

They had been sitting on the bottom for hours now. Brian had lost track of how long it had been. He had been in his cabin for a while updating his log book. Not that anyone would ever see it. He was convinced they would die where they were. But it would probably at least be comfortable. Being nuclear powered, they had power for light and heat, and the scrubbers maintained the air for them. They even had food for several months. Eventually, they would all die of starvation or by killing each other or themselves. They had pretty well exhausted all their options for getting out of this.

Brian had come back up to the control room and was in the sonar room talking to the sonar operator when a new beep came over the equipment.

"What the hell is that?" Brian asked.

"Crap," the operator said. "It looks like the attack sub is still alive, and they had just drifted into a position to fire. It's a torpedo. Headed straight for us."

"What a fitting end to this little trip," Brian said. "It's not like we can do anything about it."

Haskins came over when he heard them talking about a torpedo.

"What? Now they shoot at us?" he asked.

[146]

"I think they just now drifted into the right position," the sonar operator said.

"What's the intercept time?" Brian asked.

The operator took a couple of readings and consulted his computer.

He looked at Brian and said, "about two minutes."

Haskins looked over Brian's shoulder at the sonar readout. "I wouldn't worry too much about that torpedo that's two minutes away," he said pointing to the screen. "I think I would worry about what's coming in the other direction. What the hell is that?"

"I have no idea," the operator said. "I've never seen anything like it."

It filled the whole screen from side to side and the computer couldn't identify it, either. It didn't even look like a thing, a ship, or anything else. It looked more like … nothing.

"What do you mean, the computer reads it as nothing?" Brian asked.

"Just what I said," the operator said. "The computer doesn't read it as a solid mass, it says it's … nothing. I don't understand, either, but it's going to hit us in about 20 seconds. The torpedo is still well over a minute away, but this is close and moving a lot faster."

Then everything went dark.

Who Owns Tomorrow?

Chapter 12

Event minus 2 hours

DARPA Headquarters, Project Achilles

"This is Karen," she said into the telephone handset. It was still dark outside, and she must have dozed off. The telephone woke her up.

"This is Dr. Sheffield," the voice on the other end said. "We have finally recovered the message on the mirror. I'm in my lab."

Karen looked up at the clock on the wall. It read 4:00.

"I'll get General Scott and we'll meet you there," Karen said.

At least now we'll know, she thought as she headed out of the office and down the hall to General Scott's office. Sebastian jumped off the windowsill and followed, padding quietly along behind her. She couldn't help but think that this whole thing was a nightmare and she would wake up and have a good laugh about it. It just wasn't working out that way. She was still unsure if this was all somehow being caused by a variant of the virus on Brian's boat. They could all be wrong about the tachyon residue actually meaning it had traveled through time. It was all just so much speculation.

General Scott was on the phone when she got to his office. She sat in one of his comfortable guest chairs and waited, pretending not to listen. She could tell he was on the phone with Atlantic Command, no doubt talking about Brian.

"Boy, if this is what you get with that first star, I may have to rethink retiring," she said after he hung up.

"Trust me," he said, "it isn't worth it."

"Any change with the attack subs?" she asked.

"No," he said, "they still can't find the *Tennessee*."

"I told you he was good," she said, smiling. "Dr. Sheffield and his team have isolated the message, come on."

"Did he say anything about it?" The general asked as they headed down to Sheffield's lab.

"No," she said. "He just said they had recovered the message."

When they got to Sheffield's lab, he was sitting at the conference table looking at the mirror. The pieces had been assembled on a cardboard backing lying flat on the conference table.

"What the hell is that thing doing in here again?" Dr. Sheffield said and pointed behind Karen. She turned around and looked where he pointed.

Sebastian had followed General Scott and Karen all the way down to Sheffield's lab and now calmly walked past them all and hopped up onto the bookshelf. He settled down on top of the same stack of books as before.

Karen just laughed, "I think he likes you, Dr. Sheffield."

Who Owns Tomorrow?

"I guess if he stays right there he can't cause any more problems," Dr. Sheffield said.

"What did the message say?" General Scott asked.

"Take a look," Dr. Sheffield said, and pointed to the mirror. "The technique we used to scan for the tachyon residue leaves an image behind."

Karen and the general came around to the other side of the conference table and leaned over the mirror.

"I was afraid of this," Karen said. "In fact, it's worse than I thought, they even have a time in the message." She looked up at the clock. "It's 4:15 now, there's no way we can get the full shield up by 6:00."

The message simply said *Don't delay Project Achilles, no matter what happens. The shield must come up on time, at 6:00 a.m.*

"This is more explicit than even I thought it would be," General Scott said. "This implies that it shouldn't be brought up at any old time, as in *as fast as you can*, it has a specific time. Does that imply something is going to happen at 6:00 a.m. this morning that the shield can stop?"

"I would think that's the implication," Dr. Sheffield said. "Whatever happened to cause the problem in the future, apparently happens at 6:00 a.m. today."

"I had always thought the shield itself might be the problem," Karen said. "The exotic fuel we're using has never been used before, and no one really knew how it was going to react. We all knew the shield theory itself

[150]

was sound and would work, but the fuel was always suspect."

"Well," Dr. Sheffield said, "that apparently isn't the problem. Whatever the problem is, the shield is the solution."

"But there's no way now to bring it up by 6 this morning," Karen said. "There's just not enough time. And, by the way, what size are we supposed to target to stop whatever this threat is? We can't do the entire building, that was never in the plans for the first test. We simply don't have the fuel for something that large."

"So, how are we supposed to react to this message?" Dr. Sheffield asked.

"Well," General Scott said, "I think the first thing that needs to happen is we immediately suspend the virus scan in Karen's department and begin to bring everything back up." He looked over at Karen. "Does that make sense?"

"Yes," Karen said. "But we can't bring it up at all unless we finish the fueling process."

"Wait, Karen," Dr. Sheffield said. "Isn't it true that you can start the shield without the full load of fuel, and that would just restrict the size of the shield?"

"Yes, it is," Karen said. "But how would you know that?"

"I've been following your experiment from the beginning," Dr. Sheffield said, and he looked over at General Scott.

Who Owns Tomorrow?

"You always had a backup for me, didn't you?" Karen asked the general. "You don't trust anyone, do you?"

"It's the nature of the position," General Scott said. "You have to make sure you have a backup for everything."

Karen turned to Dr. Sheffield. "Doesn't give you any more of an idea of how to get out of this than me, does it?"

"No, not really," Dr. Sheffield said.

"Wait a minute," General Scott said. "What was the shield supposed to cover in the test if it had a full fuel load to get it started?"

"Probably this entire floor," Karen said.

"Restart all the servers and the fuel mixing process," the general said. "Can you load the fast-fusion reactors as you mix the fuel?"

"I suppose so, we'd never thought of that," Karen said. "This wasn't intended to be a fast start. It was going to be more of a controlled launch."

"Well, we don't have that luxury any more. Get everything started. It will give us that much more of an edge since we don't know what we're up against," the general said.

Karen walked across the hall from Dr. Sheffield's lab and got her team to restart the fuel mixing process and all the servers. By her watch, they had 90 minutes. Not much time. By the time she got back to Dr.

Sheffield's conference room, the general and Dr. Sheffield were still looking at the message on the mirror.

"You know," Karen said, walking around thinking out loud, "What about Brian?"

"What?" The general and Dr. Sheffield asked together.

"What if the virus on Brian's boat is able to infect missile control to the point it could fire one of the missiles? Could that be what we waiting for at 6:00 a.m.?"

"I doubt it," the general said. "First of all, the first four are duds with new propellant they're testing. No nuclear payload. They're set to just drop into the Atlantic after they burn off all their fuel. And even if the virus finds a live one, your shield, in its present state, won't help us much, will it?"

"No, but something could always go wrong with one of the duds. Couldn't it do a lot of damage if it went off course?" Karen asked.

"Or doesn't burn off all its fuel?" Dr. Sheffield asked. "Do we know what the new propellant is?"

"No, not at this point," the general said. "But I think that's a stretch. Do you remember what kind of destruction we saw on the first message that was sent? I think that's a little more than a dud missile could cause. This place looked like a shambles."

"Just the same," Dr. Sheffield said, "why don't you call and find out what's in that new propellant? And while you're at it, if they haven't already ordered up an AWACS out of Tinker, have them put one up. Even if some of the missiles on the *Tennessee* are duds, don't you want to know when anything launches?"

General Scott just looked at him. He never liked civilians much, and Dr. Sheffield was worse. He was a scientist who always thought he was right.

"There's already an AWACS up monitoring the entire east coast. We'll know about any missile launch activity in the entire area," the general said. "And I'll find out what the propellant is." He left the room to make a few calls.

"I don't think he likes you much," Karen said to Dr. Sheffield.

"I know he doesn't," Dr. Sheffield said. "Once they get that first star, they don't like people they can't order around."

"Are you trying to tell me something?" Karen asked.

"Yes," Dr. Sheffield said. "Don't get that first star."

"If we survive this, I was actually thinking about retiring," Karen said.

"Good," Dr. Sheffield said.

"You don't think this is just any old run-of-the-mill disaster, do you?" she asked.

"Think about it," he said, "would you and I ever attempt to contact the past and try to convince them to change what they did because a missile destroyed a building?"

Karen just looked at him for a moment, "No, I don't think so."

"So," he continued, "what? The whole complex? The whole DC area? The east coast, maybe more? The world?"

"How big do you think this is …was?" Karen asked.

"I don't know, do you? He asked.

"No, I don't," she said. "But it would take a hell of a lot to make us contact the past, even more for us to try to convince them to change something they did."

"Exactly. So," he said, "if the destruction is much bigger than any of us imagine, why do we need to make sure the shield is ready by a specific time when we all know, even us in the future, it probably won't even cover this entire floor with a reduced fuel load?"

Karen got up and paced a few seconds, thinking.

"Oh, my God," Karen said when she stopped pacing. "The shield is used in the future to cover them …, us … while they try to contact the past. That's all it's for!"

"Bingo," Dr. Sheffield said. "Give the lady a Kewpie Doll. Now, we just have to figure out what the hell happened … will happen."

Who Owns Tomorrow?

"But it's still possible that, whatever the disaster is, the full-strength shield could possibly have stopped it." Karen said.

"Yeah," Dr. Sheffield said. "I'll give you that possibility, but it's pretty thin, especially since we don't really know what it was. And at any rate, that possibility is now gone because of the virus scan keeping you off-line for so long."

"Where did General Scott go?" Karen asked.

"He went to find out what the propellant is in the test missiles your husband is going to launch," Dr. Sheffield said. "But before he comes back, look at this." He slid an open laptop over to Karen's side of the conference table.

Karen looked at the formulas and diagrams for a few minutes before saying anything.

"You figured it out, didn't you?" she asked. "You know how to send messages back in time?"

"Well," Dr. Sheffield said, "it's never been tested, but I think it should work. I've even started building the tachyon emitter we'll need to do it."

"So, you think we haven't stopped whatever the future wanted us to stop?" Karen asked.

"Do you think we have?"

"No, I don't think we've changed anything. I think everything we've done so far has been what we originally intended, except now the shield is late coming up and won't be at full power."

[156]

"I have the breakdown of the new propellant in the missiles on Brian's boat," General Scott said as he walked back into Dr. Sheffield's conference room.

At the same time from the other end of the conference room, Karen's lead technician came in and said "We're just about an hour away from bringing the shield up."

Karen looked up at the clock on the wall. It read 5:20. "This is going to be close. I'm going over to the overflow server room where the generators are, they need to be online and on standby, and I'll check out all the connections and available gas while I'm at it. Maybe I can nudge things along."

Who Owns Tomorrow?

Karen walked into a flurry of activity in her main lab area. The servers were swamped with technicians, all feverishly bringing up all the applications that controlled and monitored the shield. If this wasn't done just the right way, the shield might not come up at all. This was, after all, its actual first time up.

On the other side of the room, behind the protective dividers, three technicians were working as fast as they could mixing the toxic fuel, while two others were controlling the loading of the fuel into the fast-fusion reactors. All very carefully. This process had never actually been done before either. The fast-fusion reactors had been tested, but not with this level of fuel load.

She went back into the secondary lab area where the additional servers were. No one was there, but everything seemed to be in order. There were five 100 kilowatt, natural gas fired generators and several 500 gallon natural gas tanks in the room along with all the additional servers. All the generators were vented to the outside of the building and each one was sound-proofed. Karen had gotten a lot of grief about all the combustibles actually in a room next to the main lab, but she won that battle. The generators and their fuel source had to be inside the shield in order for it to even work. Nothing in, nothing out. They even had their own CO_2 scrubbers to clean and reuse the air inside the shield. These were all issues that needed to be worked out in great detail before the shield could actually be deployed for the first time. Until the *her* in the future stepped in, she thought they had all the time in the world. Now, apparently, they were down to about 30 minutes.

Karen followed all the cables from the generators into the main shield room and verified that they were all connected to the main control panel correctly. As soon as they fired the fast-fusion reactors to kick-start the shield, they needed to start the generators in standby mode. The control circuits would automatically switch the shield over to the generators when it was fully deployed.

Who Owns Tomorrow?

Dr. Sheffield looked at the list of ingredients in the solid fuel being tested in some of the missiles on the *Tennessee*. Nothing he saw caused him to panic right away. They were all seemingly normal, high-energy chemical compounds that had been used for a long time in ballistic missiles. Just in different configurations. All, that is, except two. He had never seen those chemical compounds before and slid his laptop over to look them up. He thought he had seem something like them before, he just couldn't remember where.

General Scott's phone rang. "Yes," he answered, "Scott here."

He listened for a few minutes, then hung up.

"Where's Karen?" he asked.

"What?" Dr. Sheffield asked. He was still trying to nail down those two chemical compounds.

"I asked where Karen was," the general said.

"She's right here, why?" Karen asked as she came back into the conference room.

"I just got off the phone with Atlantic Command," the general said. "Brian's boat has surfaced, everyone's guess is just to verify bearings, but is just sitting on the surface. It was picked up by the AWACS circling off the coast of DC."

"Where was the boat?" Karen asked.

"About 250 miles south of DC," the general said.

"What is that virus up to?" Karen asked out loud as she started pacing back and forth. "Don't you think if it was going to launch against DC it would be closer?"

"Actually, no, they need a little distance to let the missile reach maximum altitude, then descend to its target."

"So DC could have been the virus's target all along?" Dr. Sheffield asked.

"Most likely, yes, that's what the target is," the general said. "The last word was the attack subs were still too far away to do anything, but that was some time ago. All we can do is hope that Brian and the crew can disable the virus."

"But the virus doesn't know some of the missiles are duds, right?" Karen asked.

"Well, we don't know," the general said. "But, that is the consensus at Atlantic Command."

"Can the *Tennessee* launch on the surface?" Karen asked.

"Yes, it would most likely damage the boat from the heat of the booster, but it can launch," the general said.

"I guess I'm still a little unclear on how a dud missile is going to inflict so much destruction that we would entertain contacting the past to have them change what they're doing," Karen said.

Who Owns Tomorrow?

"I know," Dr. Sheffield said. "I don't understand, either. I'm going over what the new propellant is composed of and I can't see anything out of the ordinary. Except for two compounds I can't account for."

"What do you mean?" Karen asked.

"I know I've seen at least one of them before, but I can't find anything in my notes about it yet," Dr. Sheffield said. "That's what I was going over when you came back from your trip to the server room. How did that go, by the way?"

"Everything's in place," Karen said, looking up at the clock on the wall. It read 5:45. "I can't absolutely say we're going to be ready by 6:00, but it will be close. It would help if I knew what we were really supposed to be protecting with the shield."

General Scott's phone rang. "Scott here," he said. He listened for several minutes, then hung up and just sat there for a minute.

"What is it?" Karen asked.

"Brian's boat has just launched a missile," he said. "The AWACS picked it up a few seconds before the phone call."

"Do we know if it's live yet?" Dr. Sheffield asked.

"No," the general said. "That'll take a few minutes to relay that data. Until then, we just wait."

Karen went to the door and yelled across the hall, "How long?"

"At least 20 minutes, we hit a small snag. We got around it, but it cost us time," was the response.

The general's phone rang, "Scott here." He listened for a few seconds, then stood up. "It's not going all the way up, apparently, the telemetry code isn't working well. It's arcing over and headed here."

"You mean to DC?" Dr. Sheffield asked.

"No, I mean here, to DARPA," the general said. "Unless it makes another course correction, it's headed right for this building. The thinking at Command is that the virus wasn't sophisticated enough to take over the telemetry, or didn't have the time to do it completely."

"Is it a dud?" Karen asked.

"As far as they can tell, it doesn't have a payload," the general said.

"Then that's it," Karen said. "Unknown, new propellant, no warhead, headed straight for this building. Don't you get it? That's what the shield would have stopped if it had gone up on time. There has to be something in this building that is going to react somehow with that missile and cause more problems than a fully armed warhead."

"Good Lord, Karen," General Scott said. "Listen to yourself. What could be worse than a fully armed ballistic missile?"

"General, you run several major projects here and you still don't know that some of the stuff we do here could probably destroy the world?" Dr. Sheffield said.

Who Owns Tomorrow?

"What happened to Brian's boat after they fired the missile?" Karen asked right away, ignoring Dr. Sheffield's question.

"They slipped back under the surface and disappeared, we don't know what's happened to them," General Scott said. "They could be moving to a different location to launch again, or they could have recovered the boat and now they're hiding from the attack subs. There's no way to tell.

"And to you, Dr. Sheffield," General Scott said, "most of my job is administrative and if it doesn't have a direct military application, I may not be aware of all the details. I'm sure you're completely aware of everything you oversee. Right now, we have about," he looked at his watch, "10 minutes to try to figure out what kind of trouble we're about to see."

"Dr. Sheffield, did you ever track down those two compounds you had never seen before?" Karen asked.

Dr. Sheffield grumbled and pulled his laptop over to where he was and started to look through all his notes again. "Yes, in fact one of them is being used right across the south hallway, and in larger quantities than is in the missile. Something called Project Darkness. According to the project's prospectus, it is part of a block of what they're calling exotic matter."

General Scott's phone rang. "Scott," he answered. He listened for a few seconds, then hung up. "ETA four minutes, it hasn't changed its trajectory. You would almost think they wanted to send a live missile right to us."

"Why here, though?" Karen asked. "We have important projects, sure, but nothing that would warrant a nuclear strike of that magnitude."

"It's a way to target the capital without actually targeting the capital," Dr. Sheffield said. "Are we absolutely sure there's no warhead?"

"As sure as we can be until it lands," General Scott said.

"If it's a dud, it's an accident," Karen said. "The virus had no idea what was in the warhead, it didn't know Brian's boat was on a special assignment."

Who Owns Tomorrow?

Just then they heard a whistle, then a soft roar that got louder and louder, then the building shook as the missile hit. The lights went out and everyone was thrown to the floor. Karen was knocked unconscious and woke up when Sebastian started licking her nose.

"Sebastian, please," Karen said, trying to wake up while she pushed the cat away. Sebastian sat and just looked at her and purred.

Karen looked around and tried to assess the situation. Dr. Sheffield and the general were still on the floor, out cold. There were several small fires around the room and the smoke was beginning to be a problem. There were already security guards from the floor security control center trying to handle all the small fires. A couple of the walls had collapsed in the conference room and there was rubble everywhere. The fires continued to pop up no matter how many they put out. They seemed to be related to power cables that were exposed when some of the walls collapsed.

The general groaned, rolled over, and sat up. He looked around and said, "Well, we know where the missile is now." He got up and tried to bring Dr. Sheffield around. The building groaned like a wounded animal, and they thought the walls were going to cave in for a moment, but it finally settled down.

"That was close," Karen said. "Almost like it was right here on top of us."

"I think it was," the general said. "Maybe right across the hall." He pointed to the Project Darkness lab. "You two stay here, I'm going to go check it out. Keep this handy," he said as he tossed a hand-held walkie-talkie to Karen.

The lights were flickering in the hallway, so the general got a flashlight from storage and clipped the walkie-talkie to his jacket collar. Across the hall from Dr. Sheffield's conference room and lab to the south was the Project Darkness lab. Its north wall had completely collapsed, and the general could see part of the body of the missile through the damaged wall.

Smoke was wafting out of the lab through the damaged wall, and there was a small fire visible in the lab area itself. He stepped through the damaged section of the wall and as soon as he got in the lab he heard a high-pitched whine coming from a table beyond where the missile had come through the ceiling.

He walked over and stomped the fire out. As far as he could see, that had been the only fire in the room. The missile was huge. Seeing it outside the confines of a submarine launch tube reinforced just how big they were.

The missile had come into the building at a slight angle and had plowed through the eight floors above them in seconds. It had stopped when the nose was driven through the sub-basement floor about eight or nine feet. By the time it stopped, the engine was sputtering, burning residual fuel off and leaking some of the solid fuel that had been turned liquid by the heat. Chunks of concrete and broken glass were on the floor everywhere and electrical conduits were sparking, thrashing about on the floor.

There had been a cabinet on the other side of the table, and the missile had grazed it and knocked it over, spilling its contents onto the table. When the cabinet fell onto the corner of the table, its electrical connection was broken and all the material in the cabinet, shielded and contained by magnetic bubbles, was no longer captive.

So, by the time the general got there, all the exotic matter in the cabinet was in the middle of the table, unshielded, and the missile was leaking now-liquid propellant into a pool that was rapidly approaching the pile of exotic matter.

The general carefully walked around the missile to the other side to the table with the neutrino emitters still powered on from the day before. They were the source of the high-pitched whine the general heard as soon as he got to the lab. He looked around for a control panel and saw it halfway across the room on the wall that had been severely damaged by the missile. He was pretty sure he couldn't turn them off there.

There was not only a high-pitched whine, but the heat surrounding the emitters was causing a shimmer effect, not unlike an oasis in the desert. The general was getting worried that they were just going to come on by themselves. There were only two of them not damaged by the missile, but they were still pointing toward the middle of the table where the exotic matter was and the liquid from the missile engine was headed.

The exotic matter, now unprotected by their respective magnetic bubbles, almost seemed to merge together into a single lump of matter that was shimmering and sparking at the same time. It was changing into something, but the general had no earthly idea what it was changing into. This was beyond anything any of them had ever seen before. While he was looking at it and trying to figure out what it was becoming, the liquid propellant pool that had been traveling toward the exotic matter finally got there. When they touched, it was quite the light show. Not sparks or fire, just a cascade of colors that would make a rainbow look tame. The general was mesmerized by it and didn't even notice that the cabinet that had originally held the exotic matter was slowly, silently, sliding towards one of the two remaining neutrino emitters.

The general was startled by the cabinet hitting the floor. It had clipped one of the neutrino emitters on its way down, and now the remaining emitter was making a soft humming sound. The high-pitched whine had disappeared, and the general was afraid it was about to fire. He had no idea what would happen with the conglomeration of material in the target area, and he couldn't figure out how to turn it off.

"Colonel Stiles, come in," he said into his walkie-talkie.

"We're here, general," Karen said. "What do you see?"

"Mostly a dud missile and a lot of damage to the building," the general said. "But that's not what concerns me. It looks like parts of the experiment they were running over here are still on and they might be reacting with some of the spilled missile propellant. I would suggest you start the process of bringing up the shield. If you started now, how long before it would be up?"

"I can't tell you that, general, you know that," Karen said. "Not only is this the first test, but it's a short fuel load to boot and once I start the process, it just comes up when it's ready. That kind of control wasn't part of the first test of the project."

"Well, dammit," he said. "just bring it up. I have no idea what's happening over here, but it doesn't look good at all."

"Okay," Karen said, "but you realize that once the shield goes up, you can't get back into this area. That wasn't part of the test, either."

Some kind of ignition was taking place on the lab table with all that now-combined matter and the neutrino emitter spewing high-speed neutrinos into the mess. But it wasn't like a normal ignition or fire. It was very different. For a moment, the general thought the table itself was being ripped apart. He could see what he thought was a dark space under the table.

"Just bring it up," the general yelled. "Now."

Karen switched channels on the walkie and said, "Hit it" to the technicians in her lab. As they started all the fast-fusion reactors, Karen watched the process on her laptop. The power levels were climbing faster than any of the simulations predicted. But, so much for simulations. They always went out the window after the first actual test. Once the fast-fusion reactors had exhausted their fuel, the shield popped on and the generators took over the load. Except for the faster power curve, it worked perfectly. She got up and intended to walk around and verify where the boundaries of the shield actually were. This was important to correlate to the fuel load they used to initiate the shield.

"General," she said on his channel. "Are you still there?"

"Yes," he said. "But I don't know for how long. Something's happening that I don't understand at all."

Who Owns Tomorrow?

"Well," Karen said, "the shield's up, so you're stuck there."

"Where is the south edge of the shield?" he asked. "Can you come see this?"

Karen had been headed across the north hallway into her lab area, so she turned around and went back through Dr. Sheffield's conference room toward the south hallway. She got to the middle of the south hallway and was stopped by the shield. The general saw her and came to the other side of the shield in the hallway.

He reached out and touched it with his palm. It was a little warm, and pulsed just a little.

"How are the walkies still working through the shield?" the general asked.

"We thought radio, light, EM, etc. would probably get through. Looks like we were right."

The general was pushing on the shield with his hand.

"Strange, isn't it?" Karen said.

"Yes, it is," the general said. "But I think that may be the only thing that's gonna save you guys."

"What are you talking about?" she asked.

He moved out of the way and pointed to just beyond on the table next to the missile fragments. "Look there, in the middle of that table."

At first, Karen didn't understand what she was looking at. It looked like someone had taken a can of black paint and painted a jagged lightning bolt on the table. But the more she looked at it, the more she realized it wasn't actually on the table, it was through it.

"That popped up a few minutes ago and has been getting larger all the time," the general said. "I have no idea what it is, but it's just now starting to exert a pull on things in the room."

"What do you mean?" Karen asked.

"It is some kind of rift to somewhere, some other place," the general said. "The inside of the rift waffles back and forth between jet black and too-bright white to even look at, so I have no earthly idea what, or where, it's opened to. For the past minute or so, it has been actually pulling in papers and pens and pencils, and now some of the chairs in the room are starting to rattle and slowly move in its direction. I can feel the pull from here, and it's getting stronger all the time."

"It looks like the rift is getting bigger too," Karen said. "It's grown another foot or two just since I've been standing here. I think you had better get downstairs and start evacuating the building."

"Karen," the general said. "There is no downstairs. Or at least there's no one there. As soon as the missile hit, everyone left the building. My guess is you guys behind the shield are what's left of the entire building."

"Well, then you had better get out while you can, there's no telling what that thing will wind up doing," Karen said and pointed to the rift.

Who Owns Tomorrow?

"Karen, don't you get it yet?" the general asked. "This is what the shield was supposed to stop. This is what you guys in the future, you and Dr. Sheffield, warned us about, but we never got the full message until it was too late. If the shield test had happened as it was originally scheduled, it would have covered almost this entire floor and would have stopped the missile before it could destroy this lab and cause this." He swept his arm in the direction of the rift. "I don't think I'm going anywhere, except maybe in there," he pointed to the rift.

"What caused this?" Karen asked.

"As far as I can tell, they left some equipment on in the lab and had some exotic matter they were working with too close to the equipment in an uncontrolled environment. My guess is it was just dumb luck that some of that material combined with the propellant in the missile and then the whole mess was hit with high-speed particles from an emitter that was left on. I doubt this was the desired effect, but it's what they got. From what I can see in here, there's no shutting this off at this point. The emitter has already powered down, so it's done its damage and the rift is still growing."

"You know there's no way we can drop the shield," Karen said. "We don't have enough fuel for the fast-fusion reactors to start them up again."

"I know," the general said. "I'm going to stay over here and report as long as I can. You need to make sure the rest of the people who are behind the shield stay that

[174]

way and stay safe. You and Dr. Sheffield need to figure out how to contact the past. After all, the disaster has already happened, this is it."

Karen said. "Dr. Sheffield has already figured it out."

"Of course he has," the general said, smiling. "Go on, go back with Dr. Sheffield and whoever else survived the strike. I'll find out what's going on in here."

Karen backed up a few feet, but basically stayed where she was. The general moved back into the lab south of the hallway and sat in one of the office chairs. Everything in that office that wasn't nailed down was shaking now, and most of it slowly moving toward the rift. It had grown while she talked to the general. It was now larger than the room itself, from top to bottom, and was at least 15 feet or so wide. The top and bottom were hidden behind the ceiling and floor, which showed no damage from it, and it was as jagged as ever. Perhaps more so. Inside the rift at this point was a bright, white light that was difficult to look at.

Everything picked up speed and continued to move toward the rift. The walls themselves buckled and the ceiling lights came down. As the rift continued to get larger, more and more of the room slid toward it. Even the missile was breaking apart and sliding toward the rift. The chair the general sat in was hit and covered by a huge piece of drywall that fell from one of the walls and that's the last Karen saw of him as the chair, the general, and the drywall slid into the rift.

She watched as all the walls, then the floor and ceiling were pulled into the rift. Then parts of the building itself broke off and sailed into the rift. As more and more of the building under and above her continued to be pulled in, she felt the shield bubble she was in tilt over violently to one side and then stabilize. She hurried back into Dr. Sheffield's conference room. There were about six or eight people there, and she could see perhaps a few dozen in her server room just beyond the double doors across the north hallway.

She went through all the screens of the shield control on her laptop and it was functioning perfectly. Dr. Sheffield was just now coming to his senses and looking around.

"What happened?" he asked.

"The missile hit the building and created some kind of rift in the lab across the south hallway. Apparently that's what the full shield was originally going to prevent if it had been brought up on time and at full strength. Now, that's what we need to convince the past to try to do."

"Where is the general?" Dr. Sheffield asked.

"I just saw him sail into the rift," Karen said. "He got caught outside the shield when it came up."

Dr. Sheffield went to the double doors that opened onto the south hallway to see the damage. By this time, half the south hallway and everything south of it was gone and the rift was getting larger all the time. It was continuing to suck in parts of the building all around them and even parts of the landscape around the building.

"How the hell are we just hanging here in mid-air while this thing sucks up everything around us?" he asked.

"I have no clue," Karen said. "I think we are venturing into an area of physics that no one has ever seen before. I suspect that if the shield is continuing to protect us from the rift, that we have reached some kind of equilibrium in space and time. Look further out, it's starting to pull in parts of the surrounding countryside."

"Let's get back to the conference room," he said. "We have a lot to do before we can contact the past."

Karen followed Dr. Sheffield into the conference room and then went past him toward her lab across the north hallway. She needed to see where the north edge of the shield was.

"Where are you going?" Dr. Sheffield asked.

"I need to know where the boundaries of the shield are," Karen said. "You know what you have to work on, I would suggest you get to it if this communication to the past is going to happen at all."

She went through her primary lab into the secondary server room where the shield generators and fuel tanks were. The north wall of the secondary server room, also the north wall of the building itself, was gone and she could see landscape and highways in the distance breaking up as it was pulled toward the rift. That wall was about 15 feet away from the last fuel tank for the shield generators. To her left, west, past the door out of the secondary server room, she could see daylight. The same thing to her right, east. It appeared that the shield was covering about half of the floor that included her and Dr. Sheffield's labs, conference rooms and offices. It was just short of where the missile actually landed. So close.

She went back through the lab and conference room to the south hallway and looked out onto the countryside and the giant, now pitch black, rift, sucking up everything in the vicinity.

It looked like the more it sucked up, the bigger it got, as she watched, several whole buildings, probably full of people, went sailing into the rift.

"My God," Dr. Sheffield said. He had walked up and stood beside her. She hadn't heard him. "Where does this end?"

"My guess is it doesn't. Look at it," Karen said. "It's getting bigger all the time. My guess is whatever this is, it's the end of everything. Remember when we were talking earlier about what it would take for us to try to contact the past and then take the unprecedented step of trying to convince them to change something they were going to do? Do you think this might qualify?"

"I would think so," Dr. Sheffield said. "Not only the end of the world, but the end of everything."

[178]

"Then I think it may be time to put your time theories to the test, Dr. Sheffield, don't you think?"

Who Owns Tomorrow?

Epilogue
Event minus 24 hours
Residence of Colonel Karen Stiles

Karen sat at the kitchen table with her morning coffee, looking out the window past the deck, relishing the new snow. It was still pretty early, at least for everyone else, and the sun was not yet fully up. Shadows were just starting to creep from the trees, and the new-fallen snow was beginning to glisten. This was her favorite time of the day, before anyone else moved and spoiled the scene. She could sit here for hours this time of year and just watch the snow and the small animals that would scurry around the neighborhood …

It seemed like it took Karen hours to get ready to finally get out of the house that morning after all that happened. All the technicians running around collecting cameras, microphones, notes, servers, and it seemed like everything else in her house, were all a whirlwind. She was trying not to think much about what she had seen, even though it seemed familiar, but it nagged at her while she was packing the car.

Dr. Sheffield told her to try to not think about it too much until they got into the office and they all had a chance to look at the recordings again. He was trying to rush her out of the house so they could all get to the office.

She had seen herself, for Christ's sake. Everyone had. And he wanted her not to think about it too much.

She had taken some time to hold Sebastian and talk to him while all the technicians rushed around gathering up all the hardware. When they were finally done, she put him in his bed and headed for the door to leave. As she got into the car, she looked around and noticed Sebastian wasn't there. For some reason, she expected him to be in the passenger seat next to her. She turned around and saw him sitting in the window, inside the house, watching her, meowing.

She started to go back to the house to retrieve him, to take him with her, but Dr. Sheffield stopped her.

"Leave him, Karen. Let's just get to the office."

Who Owns Tomorrow?

Thank you for selecting this book to be part of your Kindle or paperback library. If you like, you may send me any comments at
larry.morris.books@gmail.com

Larry Morris

Other books by this author:
The Pushed to the Stars series (3 books)
Salvage series (3 books)
Another Think Coming – the Awakening
Pathway to Anyverse
New Territory
New Territory Revealed
Close to Home

Made in the USA
Columbia, SC
07 October 2022

68671553R00100